SINK THE HOOD

SINK THE HOOD

Duncan Harding

This first world edition published in Great Britain 2000 by
SEVERN HOUSE PUBLISHERS LTD of
9–15 High Street, Sutton, Surrey SM1 1DF.
This first world edition published in the USA 2000 by
SEVERN HOUSE PUBLISHERS INC of
595 Madison Avenue, New York, N.Y. 10022.

British Library Cataloguing in Publication Data

Harding, Duncan, 1926-
 Sink the Hood
 1.   Hood (Ship) - Fiction
 2.   World War, 1939-1945 - Naval operations, British - Fiction
 3.   War stories
 I.   Title
 823.9'14 [F]

 ISBN 0-7278-5575-1

Typeset by Palimpsest Book Production Ltd.
Polmont, Stirlingshire, Scotland.
Printed and bound in Great Britain by
MPG Books Ltd, Bodmin, Cornwall.

F
1189909

Prelude to a Mystery

It was nearly dawn now.

Everywhere from the galleys to the gun turrets the sailors tensed. The 'buzz' had gone its rounds. They all knew, even in the depths of the great ship's engine room, where the motors thundered mightily, that the moment of truth was approaching. The enemy would be soon in sight.

On the bridge the admiral, legs firmly astride against the motion of the battle-cruiser going full out, eyed the heaving grey-green waste of the sea through his glasses. Around him his elegant staff officers did the same. The periodic reports from the radar operators and the engineers below came up the many tubes and were relayed to the admiral in whispered tones. It was as if they were all in some ancient cathedral, afraid to disturb its heavy brooding silence with any undue noise.

Now Admiral Holland's Number One started to count off the range, as worked out by the unseen radar operators below. "Thirty thousand . . . twenty-five thousand . . ."

The tension started to mount. Number One could feel it almost tangibly. A cold trickle of sweat started to run down his spine . . . "Twenty thousand . . ."

1

"All closed up for battle stations?" the admiral queried. His voice seemed unreal to the staff officers. It was as if another man, one they had never met before, was in command.

"All closed up, sir," Number One snapped, breaking off the countdown.

Below them in the morning gloom, the last of the deck ratings were diving for cover, dropping their brooms and pails, knowing that once the great fifteen-inch guns opened fire they'd be dead men, swept over by the mighty blast or blinded and deafened, unprotected as they were. Not far off, the fire control parties, looking like alien creatures from another world in their asbestos masks and gauntlets, crouched in the steel companionways, ready to spring into action immediately if the ship were hit.

"Eighteen thousand—" Number One broke the countdown off.

A sinister, sleek shape, heavy with menace, had slid silently into viewing range of the twin circles of glittering calibrated glass. He could hardly believe the evidence of his own eyes. It was her, all right! How often had he imprinted her outline on his mind from the recognition tables in his copy of *Jane's Fighting Ships*?

"It's the . . . the *Bismarck*, sir," he quavered, hardly recognising his own voice.

"I see her, Number One," Admiral Holland answered, in full control of himself again now. "Thank you for your identification." He adjusted the glasses with a hand that was steady as a rock. It was as if he was used to spotting the most powerful enemy ship in the world at every dawn. He nodded to his Number One.

2

Sink the Hood

No words were needed. They had all been waiting for this moment for the last thirty-six hours – indeed, an imaginative person might have said, all their lives. Number One knew what to do. He spoke hurriedly into the tube which connected the bridge with the gun turrets and those deadly fifteen-inch monsters. "Guns?"

"Sir?"

"Closed up and standing by?"

"Closed up and standing by, sir." For a moment Number One had a vision of the senior gunnery officer, dressed in his anti-flash gear and looking like some medieval knight in armour ready for the joust.

Somewhere to port, the great ship's companion warship opened fire. A silent scarlet flame stabbed the grey dawn gloom – once, twice, three times. A moment later the officers on the bridge heard the boom of the *Prince of Wales'* guns.

At once the assembled officers focused their glasses. A great splash of whirling wild white water erupted on the horizon, followed a moment later in rapid succession by a series of others.

"Missed," someone cried almost maliciously. "Not a single bloody hit."

Number One allowed himself a careful smile. The comment was typical of the rivalry existing between the *Prince of Wales*, the Royal Navy's youngest ship, and their own, the fleet's oldest.

"Give 'em a bigger firing arc," Admiral Holland decreed. "Two point turn to starboard."

"Two points to starboard!" Number One called down the tube to the engine room, as the petty officer at the

3

helm swung the 42,000-ton ship almost effortlessly to starboard.

There was no more time to be wasted. They could see the tremendously powerful shape of the German battleship *Bismarck,* a stark black outline on the horizon. She'd open fire herself any minute now and all of the British officers on the bridge knew enough about the enemy's newest ship to fear the striking power of her batteries.

"*Fire!*" Holland commanded.

"Open fire!" Number One echoed, yelling down the tube.

Below him, 'Guns' cried, "FIRE . . . FIRE . . . FIRE!"

They tensed.

For what seemed an eternity nothing happened. Then, suddenly, a hollow boom. Steel striking steel. A strange hissing sound. Gas escaping. A scratching as of a diamond on glass. A louder boom. The bridge trembled slightly. They tensed even more. Another moment. Then it would happen.

Suddenly, even surprisingly, although they knew of old what was coming, the whole of the great ship – some three football pitches in length – shuddered like a live thing. The three great guns of A turret crashed into action. Scarlet flame stabbed the gloom. The three huge missiles screeched overhead.

The men gritted their teeth. Others clapped their hands to their ears, as if afraid they would be deafened by that bansheelike howl. Here and there on the bridge officers gasped, as if they had been abruptly struck in the guts.

Another shudder. It set the plates off squeaking and

creaking in metallic protest. An instant afterwards, the B turret's guns followed with another tremendous, awesome salvo.

Great splashes of whirling white water spouted on the horizon. The *Bismarck* disappeared from sight. On the bridge officers held their breath and prayed. Could it be possible? Others swallowed hard and waited for the spouts to disappear. Then they too would be certain.

Admiral Holland kept his right cheek from trembling with an effort of sheer willpower. Was he going to go down in the history of great conflicts as the hero of the Battle of the Denmark Strait – for that's what they might call the battle if it were a British victory – or as the commander who had lost the Senior Service its three-hundred-year-old command of these northern waters? The next few minutes would tell . . .

Thus the most decisive naval battle of World War Two in the West commenced. It was five thirty-five Central European Time. The position was sixty point five degrees north and thirty-eight degrees west in the Denmark Strait. HMS *Hood*, once known as the 'Pride of the Royal Navy', and her sister ship, HMS *Prince of Wales*, had taken up the enemy challenge.

Some eight miles before them steamed the most modern warships in the world, the German battleship the *Bismarck* and her sister ship the *Prinz Eugen*. Defiantly they had thrown down the gauntlet. Now the battle of the Titans could begin.

The awesome challenge for mastery of the northern seas was under way.

5

Our Author is Exasperated

God, why am I doing this?

It's not the advance payment from the publisher. That's pitiful anyway. Besides, I've passed my three score and ten. I've got enough to last me out – and I certainly don't need the hassle, as they say today.

Surely there must be other things I could be doing in my declining years. Why should I be delving into a long-forgotten past, which as far as I can see in this 'Glorious Year of the Millennium' has absolutely no bloody relevance to my potential readers? Who cares what happened so long ago in our brave new world?

After all, there were only three survivors and since that May day in 1941 when it all took place, their relatives and those of the hundreds of dead must have long passed on, or have been locked away totally gaga in some cheap nursing home to which a thankful state – and naturally their family – have consigned them. Even if those who do not dribble food from toothless gums as they perch in their Parker Knolls with the pisspots beneath *do* remember those long-lost 'boys in blue' – those dead youths – the memories of their eternally young and cheerful faces must have long

6

been eased into the darkening recesses of their failing minds.

The place in which I write these words does not improve my mood one bit, gentle reader, I can tell you. It's one of those coastal places. You know – plenty of free accommodation in winter and cheap.

Cheap these places might be, but they do tend to be gloomy. Indeed, mostly they're bloody miserable – rooted, too, like the memory of that great ship so long ago, in a kind of faded, bitter past.

The wind off the sea is – as usual – fresh and invigorating. But the sea is inevitably grey-green, choppy and mournful. Even Nature seems to do little for these winter-forgotten seaside 'resorts'. And they're all the same, whether they're located on the North Sea, Atlantic, even the Med. In winter such places invariably smell of damp plaster, rotting underwater timbers, seaweed, and – let's face it – defeat.

Why defeat? you may ask. I really don't know. But they do. Perhaps it's due to the people who live in these coastal dumps in winter. The tourists, the drunken trippers, the screeching kids with their candy floss and rock have departed. With them they have taken the bit of rowdy, beery spunk these places possess. Those who stay on know that they have been left behind to serve a full sentence, as it were. Perhaps they're even 'lifers' bound to die here. God forbid!

I take a drink of whisky. The eternal fuel of hack writers with writer's block. It'll help for a little while. The burn in the throat often burns into the imagination, gives it a kick-start. But after a while the fuel burns up –

it always does – and the imagination stops rolling. You're back where you started.

I get up and walk to the window. It's cold outside. The panes are steamed up. I don't rub them clean. There's no need. I know what I'll see out there: the white combers curling inwards in those graceful icy rolls, time and time again, on and on, as if they'll never cease until they've washed the defiant land away for good.

Of course, I know that it's not just writer's block which is giving me the 'heebie-jeebies', as they used to say in my youth. It was the sheer bloody-mindedness of the Association. It wasn't just that I was a 'scribbler', as I heard one of the old farts say when he thought I was out of earshot – of course I am. It was because they seemed to feel that the great doomed ship belonged solely to them; as if they had an exclusive right to its story and that terrible disaster which overtook the ship in May 1941.

At first when I'd met them in the pub (and paid for several rounds of rum and coke, followed by beer chasers – old farts they may be, but they can still knock back the booze) they were just stand-offish, feeling me out, wondering what I was after. They'd nod sagely and say, when I raised a point, "Old Chalky White, now he'd have been able to tell you that, but he isn't with us any more," or "Funny you mentioned that, Mr Harding," – or 'Dunc', as some of them were calling me after the third round of double rums – "but the committee's decided we're not going to talk about that. You might not understand, not being a matelot like, but we've got to protect our old shipmates."

Afterwards, when the booze really started to talk,

they were snappy, irritable in that grumpy old man's fashion, as if I were trying to trick them, betray their 'glorious past'. One of them actually used the phrase. Christ Almighty, as if the 'glorious past' means anything in the year 2000! Most of the young people I deal with, especially in publishing for instance, don't even remember what happened yesterday in the decidedly unglorious past.

Still, as I grew increasingly hot under the collar, wishing I'd ordered a real drink instead of that paint stripper masquerading as rum the old boys were drinking, I told myself they were trying to fudge the issue – hide something.

Hadn't it been the same with the toffee-nosed civil – very uncivil really – servants of the Ministry of Defence? The archivists at Kew had been little better. Polite and as efficient as they were, they weren't releasing anything more on the subject than they had done over half a century ago. The ship and what really had happened to it seemed to be taboo subjects. All of them were hiding something, I was sure of that.

I gave the old codgers another whirl. In essence they weren't bad blokes. They were just trying to protect their 'glorious past' and cover up what really happened in 1941. So I told them my sad tale of the old woman in the slitted boots. How she came running down the passage in her dirty floral pinny and a man's pair of boots, with the sides cut open on account of her corns; how she brushed by the terrified lad from the GPO who'd brought the fatal telegram; and how she screamed and screamed and screamed yet again, "The

Hood . . . my boy's gone down with t'Hood . . . BOY
. . . GONE DOWN . . . HOOD . . ."

Even today, now that I'm old, I can still remember
how that cold finger of fear traced its way down the
small of my back as I watched, petrified, with the other
kids, that woman's overwhelming grief. I'd never seen
anyone overcome by such terrible hysteria before and
haven't seen much like it since, over the intervening
sixty years. That scene on that overcast muggy May
afternoon in the middle of World War Two etched its
way on to my mind's eye. It is there to this very day.

But my youthful memory cut no ice with the old
codgers of the Association. Perhaps they had seen worse
in their time. Perhaps it was something beyond their
comprehension. But then they hadn't gone down with her.
They had only good memories of her. They remembered
her when the ship had been the 'Pride of the Royal
Navy': the ship they sent to show the flag all over
the Empire in those halcyon days of the twenties and
thirties – all gleaming brasswork and sparkling white
decks. They were intent on preserving the memory of a
vessel in her prime, when Britannia ruled the waves and
all that sort of thing. Understandably, they didn't want
to know her blazing from end to end, all hope gone,
virtually destroyed in eight minutes' battle against the
German enemy, for which she had been preparing ever
since she had been launched back in 1918.

And of course, they certainly didn't want to hear
about their former shipmates, the survivors dying in their
hundreds in those frozen northern waters until there were
just exactly three of them left. No, naturally they didn't

wish to be reminded of that tragedy . . . *just three out of a crew of nearly two thousand* . . .

So where do I stand? It was the same question I had asked myself at that reunion of the old codgers in their neatly pressed blazers, immaculate grey flannels with all their 'gongs' polished and sparkling. Standing at the window today, staring out of it at the eternal sea, as, undoubtedly, many thousands of other lonely men and women do throughout the kingdom, I posed it yet again. It remained without answer, as it mostly does.

So why do I ask it, as undoubtedly all those other ordinary men and women do? Perhaps it is because we feel threatened by some sort of nameless doom. Why, we do not know. What that doom is, unless it's death itself, we know neither. All we *do* know, I told myself, as the soaked postman staggered up the path to the cottage, buffeted by the wind and rain, the heavy bag dragging him down at one shoulder so that he looked like a hunchback, is that we – *I* – must do something. Anything. If we don't, surely we must go under.

The postman rings the bell and I realise that events are taking a new course. They have to do so. I force a smile and hurry to the door . . .

One

"*Habt acht!*"

The harsh metallic command echoed and re-echoed the length of the quay. As they had been trained to do, the five thousand sailors, the ribbons of their caps streaming in the wind coming off the sparkling Baltic, straightened their shoulders, youthful confident faces suddenly set and determined.

The officer in charge of the great final parade bent stiffly to the microphone set up on the podium. All around were the flags of the old Imperial Navy and those of the New Germany snapping and cracking in the breeze like live things.

"*Still gestanden!*" he barked.

All five thousand pairs of jackboots stamped to attention. On the quayside the frightened gulls rose in hoarse cawing protest.

Slowly the long black Mercedes, followed by the outriders, gently revving their motors, started to roll towards the platform. Along the route, tall marines came to the present, their gloved hands slapping the wooden stocks of their polished rifles audibly. All was proud pomp and circumstance, while the sun blazed down, the sea sparkled a crisp, hard blue and in the distance, the garrison band blared out 'Preussens Gloria', the big drum thumping out the cadence like the beat of some gigantic heart.

Standing stiffly to attention, young Oberfahnrich Klaus von Kadowitz felt his heart almost burst with pride. What a spectacle they made! These men, young and as tremendously fit as he was, each man dedicated to the service of the Folk, Fatherland, and Führer; every one of them prepared to sacrifice his young life for the cause if necessary. He gripped his ceremonial dirk ever tighter, his lean face under the cropped corn-yellow hair set and determined.

Beyond, the great ships which would be soon setting sail for their first cruise against the English enemy glistened in the grey wartime paint, mighty symbols of the New Germany's power. Who couldn't fail to be proud of his country, his countrymen and the weapons of war wrought by German men and women? No wonder the Führer and his *Wehrmacht* had beaten the decadent effete French the year before. How could he not do so with such power behind him? Now, soon, it was going to be the turn of the perfidious monocapitalist English.

The Mercedes rolled to a halt. An adjutant, all lanyards and gleaming braid, opened the door for the old admiral, who had built this fleet from the shambles of a defeated, humiliated Germany back in 1919. Slowly, fumbling a little with his ceremonial sword, Grand Admiral Raeder, wearing the high, starched wing-collar of the Imperial Navy, rose.

Kapitän Horsthagen, in charge of the parade, raised

his right hand in salute and bellowed at the top of his voice so that, a suddenly amused Klaus von Kadowitz told himself, the poor old admiral must be deafened, if he wasn't deaf already.

"*Mannschaften der Kriegsschiffe* Bismarck *und* Prinz Eugen *angetreten und melden sich zur Stelle, Herr Grossadmiral*!"

Slowly, very slowly, as befitted an old and very important man, Grand Admiral Raeder, head of the German Navy, touched the rim of his brilliant, gleaming cap and replied simply, "*Danke.*"

He paused while they waited, the thousands of them hardly daring to breathe, as in the distance the brass band blared and somewhere a donkey-engine clattered on one of the Polish docks. The admiral's old eyes swept slowly around the rigid ranks, his gaze pausing every now and again, as if Raeder was attempting to etch each and every one of those keen, tremendously fit young faces on his mind's eye; as if it were important to do so; as if he might well be seeing them for the first and last time. Finally he ordered, "You may stand at ease." It was more in the nature of a suggestion than a command.

Once more the sailors' right feet shot out, hands folded behind their backs in the position of 'at ease', the movement one solid uniform crash on the wet jetty, and then utter silence. Both the band and the donkey-engine had suddenly ceased their noise. It was almost as if even the humble donkey-engine operative had realised just how important this moment was: that it was a moment of history.

"Sailors of the *Bismarck* and the *Prinz Eugen*," the

14

admiral began, voice suddenly very loud and harshly metallic. *"Kameraden!"*

It was the customary form of address, the young Oberfahnrich knew, but at this particular moment he felt that the admiral was overcome by some inner emotion, perhaps the memory of his own fighting youth, and was aware of the significance of what he was to tell them. That 'comrades' was his signal that he felt at one with them when they sailed away on the high seas to do battle with the treacherous enemy English.

"I will not waste words, comrades," Raeder continued. "Back in September 1939, at this very place, units of our High Sea Fleet took part in the action that destroyed the Poles." The old admiral could not quite resist a sneer in his voice at the mention of the inferior Slavic subhumans. "Then one of our battleships, the *Schleswig,* shattered and battered them into surrender just on the other side of that sound, which is today German again." He meant *Westerplatte,* Klaus knew, where the trapped Poles had held out for a week, some of them committing suicide before they would surrender. His handsome young brow creased in a frown. Perhaps one should not talk of one's defeated enemy like that, even if they were only 'Polacks'. They *had* been brave men.

"That ship," Raeder continued, "had been a trusty but old one, laid down before the Great War. It had triumphed against the enemy, although for some of us of the old navy it had been a symbol of our defeat and military emasculation after that war, stabbed in the back by those traitors of the Home Front. Now," his old voice rose with scarcely concealed pride, "those bad days are over. You, comrades, will go into battle not in an old keel, but in two of the most powerful and most modern ships in the world." He paused as if he expected applause, like some politician addressing a party rally.

He got it, too. Captain Horsthagen cried, *"Ein Hoch für den Grossadmiral!"* Thousands of bold bass voices rose in a hearty cheer, which once again sent the gulls rising into the May morning sky in protest. Raeder actually flushed.

Klaus von Kadowitz could have sworn that momentarily there were tears in the old man's eyes. His heart warmed to him. As the Führer had often stated, they were one great community, pulling together not for personal and selfish reasons, but for the good of the whole.

Raeder nodded his appreciation and his face grew hard and serious once more. "Comrades, many of you have never been in battle before. Now you have a chance to prove yourselves in that bloody, awesome field. Make no mistake. There is a kind of beauty in battle, but there is also that sombre reality." He paused so that his words would have full impact when he spoke them. "It is that someone – perhaps even you, yourself – must die."

At that moment, carried away by it all, Klaus was tempted to break ranks and cry with all the fervent patriotism of his young heart, "Herr Grossadmiral, we are prepared to die in battle – and die gladly – for the honour of the fleet and our Fatherland!" But he restrained himself just in time. The von Kadowitzes did not indulge themselves in that kind of showy patriotism.

For nearly three centuries the family had served Germany honourably and faithfully, ever since the days

16

of the great Prussian king, Frederick the Great. They had shared Germany's victories – and her defeats! But they had kept their feelings to themselves. After all, wasn't the family motto, engraved over the portal to their decaying, impoverished estate not far from the new border with Russia, '*Mehr Sein Als Scheinen*' – 'to be more than to appear'? Let others gain the kudos of victory – and the rewards. All the von Kadowitzes aimed to do was to carry out their duty faithfully and to the best of their ability.

"The English are defeated on land," the admiral was saying. "We all know that – thanks to our brave soldiers. But their navy is still a force to be reckoned with. Their chiefs will attempt to lure us out of our harbours and, massing their ships, which clearly outnumber ours, they will do their utmost to blow us off the high seas. But since when – in this war – have the English been calling the tune?" He answered his own question. "Those days are over. Now New Germany makes the decisions and the English dance to our tune. Now *we* decide when and where we do battle with the Tommies."

Obermaat Hansen from the *Prinz Eugen*, his rum-reddened eyes filled with unsurpressed excitement, his brawny chest, heavy with the medals of the Old War, could not contain himself any longer. He lurched out of the ranks, fist upraised in an unconscious salute from those days when he had been a brief member of the Communist Party during the Kiel Mutiny, and cried, "God bless you—"

The rest of his words were drowned by the first lowering boom of flak artillery from the west, as the twin-engined bombers came zooming in at mast height.

"Great crap on the Christmas tree," Klaus yelled, for Hansen was in his division and in a way he was responsible for the tough old petty officer – that is, if anyone could claim to be responsible for him. But he had no time to give the matter of discipline any thought, for already the fleet was taking up the challenge and the quick-firers and multiple machine guns which lined the decks of the two great ships had begun pounding away in frantic fury. In an instant the sky was full of exploding balls of angry fire and officers everywhere on the docks were yelling urgent orders for the divisions to disperse while they could still do so.

Klaus, yelling out orders, snapping to his men to dive for cover, barking directions to the quayside air-raid shelters, caught sight of the first flight of 'Tommies' coming in low. They were twin-engined Wellingtons, spread in a tight camouflaged V, their pilots guiding their planes through the lethal criss-cross of bursting flak shells and puffs of brown smoke like experts. Even at that moment of extreme tension, he told himself the English were veterans. They had come so low now that they were flying below the level of the warships' flak cannons to port and starboard. It was being left to the deck gunners armed with their multiple popguns to bring them down. And Klaus von Kadowitz knew that the Wellingtons, with their wooden latticed frame fuselage, could take one hell of a lot of punishment.

Obermaat Hansen, broad drinker's face glowing excitement, breathing rum fumes all over the younger man, cried above the boom of the flak and the deafening roar of the racing plane engines, "Them buck-teethed

Tommies are gonna get away with it! They're gonna plant one big square-egg of shit right down—"

The rest of his words were drowned by the shrill whistle of bombs hurtling down, headed right for the *Prinz Eugen,* and Klaus flung himself instinctively on to the jetty.

Just in time. The blast wave slammed against his face. He gasped for breath. The air was being sucked out of his lungs. Next moment, the concrete rose and slapped his shocked face.

"*Heil* Churchill!" Hansen cried next to him. "Buy combs, lads . . . there's gonna be lousy times ahead!"

There weren't. For in the very same instant that the *Prinz Eugen*'s gunners gave up the hopeless battle against the low-flying Wellingtons, whose prop wash was lashing the sea below them into a white-frothed frenzy because they were so low, the first of the ME-109s came zooming in at four hundred kilometres an hour, their machine guns and cannon already chattering frantically.

Klaus's heart skipped a beat as he caught a glimpse of the first fighter pilot's face behind the gleaming perspex of his cockpit. The Luftwaffe had timed it exactly right. And they had the decisive advantage. They were coming into the attack right out of the sun. The Tommy gunners were momentarily blinded.

On the wet concrete, the young sailors raised their heads and cheered like spectators at some deadly game of soccer with the home side going in for a sure goal.

The first Wellington was hit. It staggered. Desperately the British pilot tried to maintain control – to no avail. The pilot of the Messerschmitt didn't give him a chance.

He pressed his trigger once more and tracer hissed in a lethal white morse towards the stricken bomber.

Frantically the rear gunner spun his turret round. He didn't make it. The perspex of the turret disappeared behind a crazy spider's web of cracked gleaming fabric. The port engine feathered momentarily. Then it cut out altogether.

The fighter pilot showed no mercy. He fired again – carefully, aiming this time. The starboard engine was hit. The propellor sailed away seawards.

"Hard shit," Hansen cried above the snap and crackle of the merciless duel in the sky. "These Luftwaffe gents ain't got no hearts, have they, Oberfahnrich? Going to get the poor Tommy shite-hawk come what m—"

The words died on his lips. The Wellington fell out of the sky abruptly. Smoke and flame streaming from its shattered fuselage, it plunged nose-first into the boiling, white sea. No one got out.

But the English were not to give up as easily as that. Decadent though their masters might be, coming from a nation which had corrupted the world with their golden sovereigns, they were still desperately brave, Klaus could see that. Perhaps, he told himself, as he watched one of the Wellingtons heading straight for the *Mowe*, one of the escort minesweepers which was to clear the channel for them through the Baltic, this kind of thing was the last desperate fling of a nation that knew it had had its day. These brave young RAF pilots were sacrificing themselves for a cause that was already lost. It was almost as if they wished to die in the heat of battle with their blood roused rather than suffer the ignominy of the defeat that was surely soon to come.

Powerless to do anything, Klaus watched with a hypnotic, limb-freezing fascination. Next to him the hard-bitten Obermaat had pulled out a flatman filled with schnapps and was taking great greedy swallows of the fiery liquid, as if he were a spectator of some entertainment that had absolutely nothing to do with him.

By now the *Mowe* had realised the lone Wellington was heading straight for her. Her gunners opened up. At that range they couldn't miss, however wild and panicked their aim. The Wellington was being shredded in mid-air. Klaus and Hansen, surrounded by their gaping comrades on the jetty floor, gawked open-mouthed like village yokels at this duel to the death.

Still the Wellington flew on. The cockpit was shattered. A dark shape slumped forward over the controls. The pilot, dead or unconscious – it didn't matter. With grim inflexibility the Wellington came ever closer.

On the deck, some of the younger gunners had already panicked. They were abandoning their weapons as the Wellington loomed ever larger. Flame was pouring from her shattered fabric now.

Hansen groaned. "Heaven, arse and cloudburst," he shouted desperately, though no one could hear in that racket, "jump over the side . . . jump, you bunch o' frigging wet-tails!"

But it was already too late. As the starboard wing of the dying plane was ripped off and came floating and twirling down like a great metal leaf, the Wellington smashed into the side of the minesweeper. Her nose crumpled and the

21

Mowe reeled under the impact. A great searing flame tore the length of the ship like a gigantic blowtorch and, in the next instant, her gun locker went up. Small-arms tracer started to zigzag in crazy profusion into the livid sky. The minesweeper heaved and her bow reared up like a metal cliff as she broke in half. Before they could really grasp what was happening, there was one last tremendous, eye-searing flash.

Something struck the young officer a glancing blow on the side of his head. Vaguely, as if he were far, far away, he heard Hansen call, "Over here . . . over here, you slow sow-arses . . . can't yer see the frigging Oberfahnrich has been hit . . . *Los, beeil' euch, Menschenskinder.*" Then everything went black and Oberfahnrich Klaus von Kadowitz knew no more.

Two

All was back to normal in the former Polish port of Gdansk, now once more the German Danzig. Outside the great ship, there was the sound of a riveteer's hammer, echoing like that of an irate woodpecker. Fire control parties swabbed down the jetty with their hosepipes. Trucks bearing ever-fresh supplies for the fleet weaved their way in and out of the controlled chaos. Now the only sign of the terror which had recently taken place in the naval harbour was the scorched quay and the neat line of blanket-covered dead on stretchers waiting to be transported away.

Grand Admiral Raeder nodded silently, as if in approval of what he saw, then turned to Admiral Lutjens, a shaven-headed man who was tough looking in a professional, controlled manner, as befitted a senior naval officer.

Raeder said quietly, "Herr Admiral, let's go below. I have a few words to say to you still before I leave again for Berlin – and the Führer." He added the last words with a slightly sour smile, as if Lutjens must realise they conveyed more than he could express openly in front of all these officers, officials and flunkeys.

Lutjens, the fleet commander, gave a slight, stiff bow,

but his face expressed nothing – neither approval nor disapproval. Instead he said in his harsh North German accent, which revealed he came from this same Baltic coast, "As you wish, Herr Grossadmiral."

A few moments later, the *Bismarck*'s main ammo lift had taken them to his state cabin, where white-jacketed mess stewards waited with their silver trays at the ready under the eagle eye of a chief steward petty officer. Again Lutjens nodded in that stiff awkward manner of his, as if his whole body was worked by tightly coiled steel springs.

"*Getranke, meine Herren?*" the chief steward queried and without waiting for a reply indicated that the waiters should step forward. Swiftly they went from guest to guest, handing them the chilled glasses of ice-cold Steinhager, the rims of the glasses stiff with sugar as if it were frost.

Raeder raised his glass, held at the level of his third tunic button as naval tradition prescribed. "*Prost, meine Herren . . . Ex!*"

"*Prost,*" a dozen self-important voices echoed.

As one they drained their glasses, again in the traditional naval fashion.

Lutjens' hard face above the Knight's Cross revealed nothing. The others had flushed momentarily as the strong alcohol had burned its way down their gullets. Not the Vice-Admiral. He might just as well have swallowed water.

"*Wegräumen!*" he snapped at the chief steward petty officer.

In an instant the waiters, the glasses and bottles had

24

vanished, as if by magic. They might well never have even been there. Raeder sat down gratefully. Now Lutjens could see just how old the C-in-C was. He seemed to have aged ten years in the ten months since the fleet had last been engaged in the Reich's invasion of Norway. He could guess why. It was the constant fight to keep an active fleet of surface ships. He knew that Hitler thought that Doenitz's U-boats could do the job for him in the battle against the English more effectively than Admiral Raeder's new surface fleet.

"You know the general picture," Raeder commenced. "And you know the Führer's attitude." He looked to left and right, as if he half expected a Gestapo spy might well be listening to his words for any hint of treachery.

Lutjens frowned. Why didn't Raeder have the courage to stand by his convictions and stand up to the Führer? If Vice-Admiral Doenitz had his way, all the Kriegsmarine's great new ships would be damn well mothballed or turned into steel to make more of his shitty U-boats. But he kept his peace and listened.

"You are all aware of our basic problem. It really is twofold," Raeder continued. "We must convince the Führer that our battle fleet can hit the English hard. But our individual raiders, even if they are powerful ships which outgun and outspeed the Tommies, cannot tackle the English convoys without risk – and the Führer will not tolerate the loss of one of our great ships. We all know his reaction to the loss of the *Graf Spee* in '39."

There was a murmur of agreement and understanding. The Führer had gone into one of his frightening rages when he had heard that the Pocket Battleship, as the

English called the German ship, had been trapped in South America by the English fleet and would have to be scuttled if it were not to fall into enemy hands.

"So the plan is to assemble a fleet of our own powerful enough to tackle the English convoys even if they are escorted by capital ships and are within sailing distance of English Home Fleet at Scapa Flow. That is what we have been trying to do for the last few months."

He let his words sink in. Outside the sirens of the ambulances wailed dolefully as they came to collect their cargo of death. Lutjens frowned at the thought of those dead young men, killed before they had the chance to live. But the admiral told himself that it was no use, served no purpose, to dwell on such matters. There would be many other such young men dead before all this was over.

Raeder must have taken the look on Lutjens' face for one of disapproval, for he said, "I know, my dear Lutjens, you wish this operation to be cancelled until we are fully, one hundred per cent, ready to meet the English in battle. But that can never be. There will never be a time when we are completely prepared to tackle them. You see from this raid today that they are aware we are up to something. There was a similar raid on the *Scharnhorst* and *Gneisnau* at Brest last week. They are trying to knock out our ships before they even sail."

Lutjens wasn't about to cross swords with the Grand Admiral. He knew better than that. If he did he'd be dismissed and then some hack would take over and do anything that the Grand Admiral required, regardless of losses. "It is a question of an appropriate target, Herr

Grossadmiral," he commenced, his voice purposefully neutral and without emotion. "We need to plan better where we are to strike the—"

"In the terms of this operation," Raeder interrupted him firmly, "the sands are running out, Lutjens. You know the business with the invasion of Russia. The Führer is impatient to deal with the English problem before he turns his full and complete attention to the east."

Lutjens gave one of his stiff, wooden nods and lapsed into silence. He knew there was no use persisting. Raeder was carrying out orders – *the Führer's orders* – and that was that. End of message.

"Let me sum up then, gentlemen," Raeder said with an air of finality. "Once we march east, we of the navy shall receive no more top priorities. I know that we are not ready. We haven't managed to get the *Scharnhorst* and the *Gneisnau* out of that little trap yet, and it might take some time before we do so. But under present circumstances – which are not in our favour, I must emphasise – an eighty per cent readiness is better than none."

"So the operation is as scheduled, Herr Grossadmiral?" Captain Lindemann, the commander of the *Prinz Eugen*, rasped. As usual he wasted no words.

"Yes," Raeder agreed. "Operation Exercise Rhine will commence exactly as planned. The fleet will sail from here on the evening of May 18th. The Baltic will, as you know, be cleared of all merchant shipping, including that of neutral Sweden, to ensure that your ships are not observed moving westwards. Two days later you should be well into the Skagerrak before you're sighted. By then we can confidently hope that it will be too late for the English to assemble an attack force to engage the fleet. With the smallest bit of luck we'll have found our own target by then . . ."

Lutjens was no longer really listening. Raeder's plan had as many holes in it as a piece of Swiss cheese. Two days in the Baltic, normally filled with Swedish ships supplying the Reich! Even if they did manage to convince the neutral Swedes to run for harbour while the fleet passed up the inland channel, bound for the North Sea, their captains would be suspicious. They'd know there was something going on. The whole complex harbour-and-customs clearance operation that allowed them to enter German ports would tell them that. And although the Swedes were overwhelmingly pro-German, there were enough British agents in Stockholm to pass on the captains' suspicions to the British Admiralty. No, he told himself, suddenly sunk in a gloomy reverie, filled with dark and sinister forebodings, things were not going to work out. He knew that in his bones.

Admiral Lutjens raised his head and suddenly caught a glimpse of himself in the wardroom mirror opposite. He caught his gasp of shock just in time. Staring back at him was a death mask . . .

Up on the deck, saluting Grossadmiral Raeder, as rigidly at attention as if he were still a fresh-faced cadet, Captain Lindemann was still shocked by that look on Admiral Lutjens' face which he had glimpsed reflected in the mirror. What had been going through the fleet commander's mind at that moment? he asked himself as, to the shrill tune of the bosuns' whistles, the elderly C-in-C proceeded down the gangway towards the waiting Mercedes, which would take him back to Berlin and – naturally – the Führer.

Lindemann could only guess. But the result didn't please him one bit. It had been nearly a quarter of a century since the Battle of the Skagerrak where he had had his first taste of action – and he didn't like the idea of it any more than he had done as a young naval cadet back in 1916. Not only did a sailor face shot and shell like a soldier in the line, but he also was confronted by the possibility of a lonely, slow death in the water, with not a soul to hear his last prayer. Lindemann shook his head as if to ward off that fearsome vision and told himself that whatever happened now, he was not going to waste his ship and the lives of her crew. He and they would survive. What did they say: *"Die* for your country? No, *live* for it!"

Three

"*Armer kleiner Mann*," the Polish whore said softly. She raised her hand from Obermaat Hansen's lap to dab the blood still trickling from his head wound. "Let me soothe you, my little snuggle-puppy."

"Snuggle-puppy yer mitt back on me lap," Hansen barked. "That'll soothe me more, I can tell yer. My senses is coming back. Keep up the good work, and I'll give yer a real diamond-cutter, if yer lucky."

Anna Olga Dora, known in the trade as AOD, laughed wearily in that tired 'seen it all; done it all' whore's manner of hers and did as the tough old sailor requested. She wondered, as she did so, if men kept a stiff 'un even after they'd snuffed it. They always seemed to have one in her long professional experience.

Bei Anna was a typical sailors' waterfront bar. A zinc-covered table, usually awash with suds and schnapps. A dirty picture, curling at the yellow edges, of two women with cropped hair doing something impossible to each other. A fly-blown reproduction on the wall, depicting a curly-haired blond youth in an old-fashioned sailor suit urinating into a pool of water with the legend beneath it warning, "Don't Drink Water! Kids piss in it!" Next to it was a large sign in Polish and German advertising 'Pivo Krakov – Makes Strong Men Stronger'. That and the usual collection of drunks, misfits and morose young sailors crying into their beer with homesickness made up the bar's decor, plus, naturally, AOD, the regular Polish whore.

"What do you think is going to happen?" AOD asked in her harsh Silesian German. She had been born a German, but was of Polish ancestry. Her names came from the old imperial princesses Anna, Olga, and Dora. But she was Catholic, which indicated to Hansen, who was no fool, drunk as he was most of the time, that the family was basically Polish. Those who wished to be taken for pure Germans had usually converted to Lutherism back in the nineteenth century. So, although he didn't quite trust the whore – only a fool would trust a whore whatever her nationality – he liked her. Often when he was stony broke in between pay-days, she'd give him a free 'rub-off,' or if she was particularly generous even let him dance a 'mattress polka' with her in the squeaky old brass bed upstairs, where she took her regular clients to copulate under the cheap reproduction of the saintly Black Virgin of Krakow.

"Happen?" he echoed a little morosely, taking a careful sip of his Pivo Krakov, for he was about broke again, "the usual. The big shots'll decide that it's time us poor sailor lads went and got our frigging turnips blown off again. They ain't won many medals of late."

She gave his penis an encouraging squeeze through the thin serge of his trousers and smiled her gold-toothed smile at him. "Never say die," she said without thinking of her words. She licked her pink tongue around her broad generous lips so that they gleamed an inviting red. "Play your cards right, old house, and I might give you something special when you've finished your beer."

"Yeah," he said gloomily, finding it hard to shake off his mood, "like frigging leprosy, perhaps." He sniffed. "Besides, that kind of piggery costs extra, don't it?"

Her professional smile grew ever larger. "For you, my little cheetah, if you're good to old AOD, it comes free."

Hansen lowered his glass of beer with a bang on to the zinc-covered bar. The barman looked up sharply, hand flying to his mouth with alarm.

"*Free!*" Hansen cried and wished, next moment, that he had not spoken so loud. Something like a sharp wire had bored itself into the back of his right eye with a stab of red hot pain. "Frigging wonders never frigging cease."

Now she laughed and squeezed his penis even harder. "Nothing's too good for our boys in the service." She used the old phrase.

Before he could react with the usual contempt he felt on hearing the propaganda phrase, the tinkling bell of yet another convoy of ambulances heading for the *Marinekrankenhaus* started to race by in a great hurry, scattering the Polish dock workers coming off shift and weaving in and out of the blue-and-white trams dangerously. Hansen frowned as he spotted the scarlet drops of blood coming from the rear of the boxlike contraptions. Next to him, AOD crossed herself in the elaborate Polish Catholic fashion. "Poor boys," she exclaimed.

Obermaat Hansen didn't comment. He was a hard-bitten old salt who had seen some rotten things in his time, during two major wars. Yet the thought of young men dead for a cause that they didn't, perhaps, understand or which meant nothing to them always affected him. "Full of all that piss and vinegar, mates," he would comment to his fellow petty officers when the subject was sometimes raised, "and buggered without ever using it."

He looked at himself sombrely in the fly-blown mirror at the very same instant that the thick felt curtain, which functioned as a blackout after dark, was thrust aside to admit two middle-aged men with their felt hats pulled down far over their faces.

AOD's hand holding his penis gripped so hard that Hansen almost yelped with the sudden pain. He knew why. The two middle-aged civilians were cops. They had Gestapo – Secret State Police – written all over them: the hats, the long green ankle-length leather coats, the super-cilious look on their evil mugs. No, there was no mistaking them. They were the frigging Gestapo all right.

"Funny pong in here suddenlike," Hansen said aloud. "Wonder if that frigging roof hare" – he meant a cat – "bin pissing on cops' boots again? I suppose," he added with studied insolence, "that it's only right that they piss on cops."

The bigger of the two, his metal identification disc in his hand, flushed an ugly red and snarled, "You're risking a thick lip, sailor – and worse." The threat was undeniable.

It didn't worry Hansen. He knew he could say what he liked *now*. As torpedo-room senior mate, the *Prinz*

Eugen's skipper wouldn't let the Gestapo do anything to him. The armoured giant needed him now that they were going into action at last.

The thought emboldened Hansen. Besides, he was slightly drunk and he had never been frightened of cops even when he was sober. "Oh dear, oh dear, woe is me," he simpered in what he imagined was a female falsetto. "I do think I'm gonna faint the way that naughty policeman is addressing me."

Some of the older sailors in the bar laughed until a look from the bigger cop wiped the grin from their faces. Next to Hansen, AOD pressed his penis even harder.

"Knock it off," she hissed urgently, and there was no denying the fear in her voice now, "you'll only get us into trouble. Leave it be and I'll be especially nice to you – you know how."

He looked at the still handsome woman. There was genuine fear written all over her broad slavic face. For a moment he wondered why. AOD was not usually afraid of the law. She paid them their monthly bribe and when necessary she granted extra favours. Why should she be afraid?

He had no time to dwell on the answer to that unspoken question, for the cop he had insulted creaked closer in his heavy boots and hissed, "All right, arse-with-ears. Get the dirty water off yer chest with that pavement pounder of yourn and then back to your ship while you still can." He thrust his ugly mug forward threateningly.

A hot retort sprang to Hansen's lips, but he didn't utter it. The whore cut in with, "Come on, lover boy. You've paid your money, let's get it over with." She dragged at his brawny arm almost angrily.

The cop sniggered. "Watch he don't come all over yer belly, Anna. These sailor boys don't know no discipline. Yer wonder why they waste their money in knocking shops. I mean – the five-fingered widow could do it for them for nothing." He made an explicit gesture with his clenched fist and burst out laughing.

Red-faced, Hansen allowed himself to be dragged to the stairs behind the bar while the cops, still laughing at their great sense of humour, as they supposed it to be, started to examine the other occupants' papers.

Hansen waited until he and Anna started to clump up the creaking wooden steps that smelled of stale sweat and ancient lecheries before snorting, *"Du machst doch in die Hose, Mädchen!* Why are yer worried about them two flatfoots? You know they're both blowhards. Besides they need the bribes they got off'n you pavement pounders to pay their old women back home in the Reich."

Before she answered, Anna looked fearfully behind her, as if she were afraid the cops might be listening at the bottom of the dark stairs. "It's not that," she said. "There's something going on."

"What?"

"It's something to do with the bombing of your ships a bit back."

"Shit on the shingle!" Hansen cursed. "You're talking like a five-groschen novel, Anna. Talk some sense, wench."

She looked at him. Abruptly the fear had gone. It was dark on the stairs and he couldn't see her face very clearly. Yet he sensed somehow that there had been a change in her expression: a new quality of proud defiance which he had never encountered in her before – or in any other cheap whore like her, for that matter. "You're asking too many questions," she said quietly, the fear vanished from her voice now. "People who ask too many questions can get themselves into trouble."

"And what's that supposed to mean?" he demanded, surprised.

She didn't answer his question. Instead she said, pulling him round the corner to the untidy bedroom, "Come on, get your pants down and get on with it. There isn't much time left."

Obediently he did as she commanded. There wasn't, and, as he had confessed to his fellow petty officers that very morning, "Comrades, I've got so much ink in my fountain pen, I don't know who to frigging well write to first." But later, when he was on his way back to the *Prinz Eugen*, with uniformed cops and naval sentries everywhere, he considered her phrase once more. What had she meant – 'There isn't much time left'? For *who*? And *what*?

Four

The Führer farted.

His facial expression didn't change. But then he farted all day long and was no longer aware of the fact. It was due to the vegetarian diet he preferred and the laxatives he swallowed constantly to keep down his weight. But if Adolf Hitler wasn't aware of his wind-breaking, those around him were. Their faces went pale. Even Blondi, his Alsatian bitch, whimpered and fled into the corner, tail between her legs.

Next to Canaris – the head of the Abwehr, the German Secret Service – Admiral Raeder flushed and whispered out of the side of his mouth, "The man's impossible. Breaking wind like that – and ladies present." He indicated the two young female secretaries poised next to Bormann of the Reich Chancellory, their notebooks at the ready.

Admiral Canaris, sallow-faced, small and secretive, made no comment. He rarely did. As head of the German Secret Service, he made it his policy to say as little as possible in public. It was better that way. He had too many enemies. It was wise not to give them any possible ammunition they might use to shoot him with.

The Führer beamed as if he had achieved something of importance. The fart had eased the usual turmoil in his guts temporarily, Canaris told himself, but in five minutes or so he'd fart again. After all, he, Canaris, should know. Naturally he had a file on the Führer, which included details of both his unusual sexual habits and the state of his unruly, gas-filled guts.

"*Meine Herren*," Hitler greeted the two admirals, as if they were the oldest of friends, though in fact he had very little time for them and their Navy. After all, he was an Austrian, who had never even seen the sea till he was in his late thirties and who was seasick as soon as he stepped on a boat, even when it was safely at anchor in some protected harbour. "Welcome."

Both of them clicked to attention and gave the master of Western Europe a stiff bow. Behind the Führer, Bormann nodded to the older of the two secretaries and stepped further into the background. As he did so, he gave the cowering Alsatian bitch a malicious little kick in the ribs. He smiled slightly, as if the action had given him some kind of pleasure.

"Gentlemen," Hitler commenced, as the secretary began to take down his every word at Bormann's instruction, "we do not need to waste any more time on Operation Exercise Rhine. It is, I take it" – he shot a sharp look at Raeder – "all taken care of?"

"It is."

"Good, Raeder. Deadline?"

"The fleet under Lutjens will leave Danzig on the tide in the evening of May twentieth under the cover of darkness. With a bit of luck, *Gneisnau* and *Scharnhorst*

38

in Brest will be ready to sail and meet them off the coast of Greenland."

"Excellent. I am pleased, Grand Admiral," Hitler said quickly and raised his right haunch slightly.

The secretary knew the movement of old. It was the signal he always gave when he was about to break wind. Discreetly she moved back a few paces and prepared to hold her breath.

"Now the question of a target . . . something which will hit the English hard before what happens in the East next month makes them believe" – he grunted and broke wind once again, his face giving a fleeting sign of relief, but no other to indicate what he had just done – "that there is still some hope for them. Churchill, that drunken sot, is a rabid anti-Soviet, a man after my own heart in some ways, but he'll make the most of the fact that the Reich will now be engaged in a war on two fronts to East and West and that this will take the pressure off his precious British Empire."

Hurriedly the pale-faced secretary, who had paused to pat her nose and mouth with her handkerchief to prevent herself from gagging at the stench coming from the Führer, attempted to catch up with one of his typical long sentences, sweating visibly.

In a way Hitler answered his own question with, "Naturally we can destroy one of their convoys. Even with just the firepower of the *Bismarck* and *Prinz Eugen*, should the Brest ships fail to make the rendezvous, the fleet would be able to make short work of a collection of merchant ships and destroyer escorts. But is that enough,

I ask you gentlemen?" He searched the two admirals' faces with his piercing hypnotic gaze.

Raeder opened his mouth, presumably to defend his fleet and say that it was. The humble little head of the Secret Service in his shabby uniform and dingy gold insignia beat him to it.

"There is a possibility of a great naval victory, *mein Führer*, if luck is on our side," he said softly. "Luck is the vital element, I repeat."

Hitler's sombre face lit up. He even forgot the noisy rumblings in his stomach, which sounded like a drainage system that had gone seriously wrong and badly needed urgent dismantling. "Go on," he urged. "Tell me more, Canaris." He grinned. "I know your devilish mind. What arcane trickery have you dreamt up now?"

Canaris was not impressed. Indeed, he wished he was not being forced – due to Raeder's predicament with the Brest ships – to disclose his plans. After all, he trusted no one, not even the Führer. He preferred to fight his battles, dirty and underhand as they mostly were, in the shadows where they belonged.

Instead of looking directly at the Führer who stood there, waiting in eager anticipation for whatever surprising rabbit his head of the Secret Service was about to produce as if from some magician's top hat, he stared numbly at his feet and mumbled, "*Mein Führer*, it is a combination of English pride centred on an eighteenth-century British admiral of theirs; English cheapness; and love for short-term results – and a fat lady, who, supposedly, is a medium with an excellent ability to raise the spirits."

Sink the Hood

The Führer's mouth dropped open. Behind him the secretary broke the point of her stenographer's pencil with surprise, and Admiral Raeder exclaimed, flushing a brick red above his old-fashioned stiff collar, "What in three devils' name are you talking about, Canaris? . . . My God, man," he spluttered, hardly able to find the words to express his exasperated bewilderment, "you're talking in riddles!"

Canaris kept his head bowed, a lock of his snow-white hair – which had earned him the nickname of 'Father Christmas' among his enemies of the Gestapo – falling over his brow, and let the wave of shocked surprise run over him. But his cunning devious mind was racing electrically as he did so.

Suddenly Hitler was intrigued. He clapped his hands. Bormann emerged from the shadows at the back of the great hall immediately. *"Mein Führer?"*

Hitler didn't even look at the servile secretary with the face of a boxer gone to seed. "Tea for myself and coffee for the gentlemen," he ordered. "I believe that Admiral Canaris has an interesting tale to tell. Let us take some time to enjoy it. Ensure that my other appointments are postponed for at least thirty minutes."

"Jawohl, mein Führer. Zu Befehl."

Five minutes later they were all ensconced in the *Sitzecke* – the 'sitting corner', as the Germans call it – drinking tea and coffee, plus *Enzianschnaps*, the Führer's own favourite tipple made from herbs, served by jackbooted, white-clothed SS giants. They looked for all the world like a cosy little group of middle-class folk enjoying the traditional German *Kaffeeklatsch*.

41

Swallowing yet another *Pfefferkuchen*, Canaris, who enjoyed his food, licked his fingers and prepared to relate his story: one that indirectly would result in the tragic end of a great ship and the death of nearly two thousand British seamen . . .

"So," Canaris said, as the old clock in the corner next to the *Sitzecke* ticked away the minutes of their lives with metallic inexorability, "you can see, *mein Führer*, why the English wanted to give the name of that eighteenth-century admiral to their newest and most powerful ship back in 1918."

"*Natürlich*," Hitler agreed, taking another delicate sip of the peppermint tea that his doctors had recommended to soothe his upset stomach, which was beginning to gurgle yet again in an alarming manner. "He was a typical pirate disguised as a naval admiral. I wish that more of my own admirals were like that – not so cautious." He looked pointedly at Raeder. The latter went brick red again.

"But what of the ship named after him?" Hitler continued and belched, again without appearing to notice.

Cautiously, on her stomach, ears flat against her skull in fearful anticipation, the Alsatian bitch Blondi started to crawl out of range. She knew, apparently, what was soon to come.

"She is regarded as the pride of the English navy," Canaris answered. "And indeed, she is a fine ship."

Hitler waved his hand impatiently and Canaris speeded up his explanation, suppressing his inner annoyance. Like all officers engaged in his type of work, he loved the oblique approach. He hated to have to state facts plainly and swiftly. Still, Hitler was the chief. Not only that.

He held the power of life and death over his subjects. "She gained her reputation in the twenties with overseas cruises, showing the flag across the British Empire or being engaged in goodwill cruises to North and South America. But she *had* – and *has* – a fatal weakness."

"It is?"

"She was designed as a battle-cruiser. She sails at a top speed of thirty-two knots. She can deliver an impressive weight of shell. But, *mein Führer*, she hasn't got the armour to withstand the kind of firepower that – say – the *Bismarck* could bring to bear on her – and you will remember, *mein Führer*, that forty per cent of the *Bismarck*'s displacement is made up of her armour."

"In short," Hitler concluded, proud as always of his ability to absorb, understand and use statistics, even those that concerned a navy that he didn't particularly like, "the *Bismarck* can give *and* take punishment?"

"*Genau, mein Führer*," Raeder butted in proudly, as if he personally had been responsible for the *Bismarck*'s performance.

Hitler was thoughtful for a moment, then he said, beating Raeder to it, "So this is the ship – the pride of the English navy – that we intend to knock out?"

They nodded in unison.

"But, gentlemen," Hitler protested, holding out his arms hugely, as if he were addressing a party rally at the annual Nuremberg meetings, "how can we be sure that this paragon of the English will be there and take up the challenge when our own fleet sails to do battle?" Then he had it. "You mean the fat lady, Canaris . . . the one with the ability to raise the spirits?"

43

Slowly and apparently reluctantly, almost as if he did not wish to impart this secret information even to the Führer, Canaris replied, "Yes, you are right, sir."

Hitler smiled and, raising himself excitedly, snapped, "I knew it . . . I knew that was the surprise you were going to spring on us, Canaris."

In his triumph that he had caught the head of his Secret Service out, he forgot himself. His bottom erupted in a tremendous burst of wind. The huge fart caught even Martin Bormann by surprise. Trying to get out of the way, he stumbled over a cowering Blondi and sprawled full length, his normally ruddy features turning a ghastly green as that noxious wave overtook him.

A Message from the Other Side

The package was big and clumsily wrapped. Instead of tape to seal the old envelope, which was being used for the third or fourth time to judge by the varied stamps and cancellations, the Australian had got the post office people to stick it up with odds and ends of stamp paper. And someone had added – as further protection against the package opening – a piece of twine, wrapped around a couple of times like people used to do when I was a kid more than half a century ago.

Surprisingly enough it was correctly addressed – *completely*, down to the local postcode; and – surprise, surprise – the sender had got an 'esquire' on my name, and got it right, too. It wasn't the kind of sloppy usage you receive even from solicitors these days, such as 'D.E. Harding, Esq', but the really one hundred per cent formula of 'Duncan Edward Harding, Esq.'

Everything was explained a few minutes later after I'd managed to get the bloody thing opened, had read the first couple of lines and had recognised the spiky, shaky handwriting for what it was – that of an old man – an Englishman, naturally – who had probably learnt how to address a letter of that kind at his prep school before the Second World War.

"Dear Mr Harding, I have been advised by our national association of ex-naval servicemen of your interest in a certain wartime subject," the first sentence ran in that old man's old-fashioned style.

> By birth I am not an Australian but an Englishman from the Bath area and during the war I was a junior officer in Naval Intelligence (under Lt Commander Ian Fleming, the author of James Bond who as you know was in the same service) . . .

I sighed. The old man's writing, the mention of the fact that he was born in Bath and the name-dropping of James Bond's creator all told me one thing. I was in for a lot of long-winded pomposity from the old fart. I sighed again and looked out of the window. It was still bloody raining and at this particular moment the letter and the rest of whatever the package contained were the only leads that I possessed. I'd drawn blanks with all the old chaps of the ship's associations and even the editor of the *Navy News*, who was usually so obliging in such matters, had been of no help. Perhaps the fact that the 'man who had known Ian Fleming' (as I was beginning to call the new Australian in my mind) had lived in Oz so long might have rubbed off. Despite his prose and all the rest of it, it was possible that he would be more forthcoming.

Another sigh and I bent my head to the letter once more, screwing up my eyes in the fading winter light, with the sea thundering outside, and read on.

46

It wasn't that I was on duty when I first came across the woman – far from it. In fact I was on leave. I'd been blitzed in Portsmouth – 'Pompey' we used to call it in those far-off days – and I'd cadged a lift to Plymouth. Out of the frying pan into the fire, one might say . . .

"One might," I said to myself, "you silly old arsehole." Like most lonely people and would-be writers (remember this, as a writer you're on your own, mate. Forget the glamour. It's all toil, sweat and tears all on your ownsome, and piles from too much sitting if you're unlucky) I talk to myself.

"But I won't bore you with too many details," he'd written, as I read on.

When you get to my age your hand aches with the effort of too much writing. So I've decided to make it simpler for me – and I hope you. I'm enclosing a little piece I did for the *Alice Springs Advertiser*. It was about time the local TV did a repeat of Shute's *A Town Called Alice* and they were interested, for a time, in the Second World War . . .

I skipped the rest. I could guess it'd be pretty much the same as the beginning of the letter . . . more bull. Instead I opened the old newspaper carefully. The date was June 1990 and the headline, if you can call it that, read: 'The Spy Who Spied On Spies – A Strange Carry-On In Wartime Britain'.

I grinned at that 'Carry-On'. What with the main title and that wording, you could have expected Sid James' lecherous old face beaming out at you from the unfolded page or Barbara Windsor exhibiting her undeniable assets in one of those movies of the same name which keep appearing on our television screens, week in and week out.

Instead of those well-known comedians, I was confronted with a badly blurred picture of that old-fashioned warship that had been bothering me ever since I allowed my publisher to talk me into the book over one of his celebrated liquid lunches. He might be tight with his pennies as far as authors' advances go (but then I guess all authors say that) but he certainly doesn't stint on his lunches. It had been the Gay Hussar, full of the usual Labour politicians busy at the place's celebrated trough. But despite the 'names', the Gay Hussar's waiters had been particularly deferential to Sir. They should. My publisher usually left a lot of money in the restaurant.

Yes, there she was, looking as powerful and somehow sinister in a lean rakish manner as she must have looked back in 1918 when taking part in a war that was already finishing. I'd got a lead at last!

The man who'd known Ian Fleming's first few sentences, as carried in that obscure Australian newspaper, probably now defunct, confirmed that it was not only a lead, but one that was going to guide me down the path that I had already visualised for myself when my publisher had first dangled the project under my nose over a fiery paprika goulash, washed down with expensive Tokay.

Sink the Hood

In the winter of 1940–41, as an active officer of the Royal Navy's Intelligence Service, I was instrumental in bringing to book a woman, who ought, in some people's opinion, to have been shot as a German spy. I have no hard evidence now (nor even had then, for that matter) that she was. But it seemed to me that it was an amazing coincidence that a mere two months after she made her prediction, that great ship was hit by the Huns and by some apparent fluke, though we later learned it wasn't a fluke at all, went straight to the bottom of the sea, taking with her the whole of her crew – near two thousand of her poor chaps. Only three survived, more dead than alive . . .

I stopped there. I felt my heart race. It's something like the flood of adrenalin when your blood's up, or perhaps after a hit of whatever crappy drugs people shoot, but that's the feeling for a professional writer when he finds a lead. And I thought my new Australian, Lt Timothy de Vere Smythe (he would be called 'de Vere Smythe' – that name must have gone down like a bomb in Pom-hating Oz) had just given me that lead because there, halfway down the newspaper clipping, I'd caught a glimpse of that fat pudgy face raised on Scotch porridge – and probably Scotch whisky later on. There was no mistaking her. I'd known about her virtually from the start of my investigations but I'd given up hope of ever finding out any more about her. The whole bad business was so long ago, amid the confusion of wartime, with records in the UK being destroyed left, right and centre by Goering's Luftwaffe.

But there she was under that cliché of a title, 'The Spy Who Spied On Spies'. One didn't need a crystal ball to figure out who our tame ex-officer in the Royal Navy had been spying upon – Madame Clarissa Campbell, once known in the halls of the North of England as 'Florrie Future'. She was the spy he had seen involved with, that was for sure. But how had he known she was a spy?

I looked at the bottle of Scotch. Should I? I decided not to. What I was now going to read slowly and carefully should be stimulation enough. I settled myself in my chair more comfortably. Outside the wind howled and the sea thrashed, the shingle slithering back and forth noiselessly. But I was no longer listening. I was preparing myself to slip back into that long-forgotten world of England at bay, circa 1940–41. That would provide all the intoxication I needed now . . .

Five

De Vere Smythe needed a change of underclothing, a stiff drink and, if he were exceedingly lucky, a nice nubile blonde in bed with him in the large double room he had managed to book for himself at a moment's notice with surprising ease for packed wartime Plymouth.

But once he had emerged from the station into the snowbound darkening street, he knew why it had been so easy. The city was virtually empty. It was obvious that the Huns had been to Plymouth quite recently. There was still smoke drifting over the city centre and here and there Civil Defence men in their blue battledress and white helmets were picking away half-heartedly at fresh ruins, looking – without too much hope – for the last bodies.

De Vere paused and looked at the green-glowing dial of his watch. What should he do next? Get cleaned up? Or should he chance his arm and hope that his uniform might win him a double whisky in the first pub he came to? Landlords were notoriously cagey with their spirits when it came to strangers, even if the stranger was prepared to pay over the odds. They hid the damned stuff beneath the bar as if every drop was exceedingly precious. All they'd give you, if you didn't persist, was the usual 'gnat's piss', as the matelots called it – mild and bitter.

Despite de Vere's gloomy predictions, he struck lucky in the first pub that he went into. The landlord looked at his weak, white-faced features, took in the soiled stiff white collar and the rings of the 'Wavy Navy' on his tunic and said, "Got a nice bit of Scotch if you fancy, sir. Just got it in from my supplier." He touched his long nose, heavy with blackheads, significantly.

De Vere jumped at the chance. The pub was run down, had not been painted for years and had sawdust on the floor. It was obviously working class, but the promise of Scotch convinced him to stay.

"Rather," he said in the affected upper-class accent he had learned at his prep school, "do give me a large Scotch, please."

"Coming right up, sir. That'll be three and six."

The price was steep, but de Vere didn't mind. He needed the drink. Besides, the only other occupant of the saloon bar, a woman – dressed in a black suit, surprisingly enough, with peroxided hair – was definitely giving him the eye via the big fly-blown Victorian mirror behind the bar. She was obviously a 'lady of the night', as he preferred to call prostitutes, but she was decently dressed and she was in the saloon bar where drinks cost a penny more than in the other, public, one.

He gave his drink a squirt of soda and raised his glass in toast to the whore looking at him in the mirror. She did not need a second invitation. She was over like a shot, uncurling her legs to reveal that above her black silk stockings she was wearing no knickers and saying in what she apparently thought was a seductive voice, "I'll have a gin, if it's all right with you, duckie."

It was.

"Thus it was that I met the unfortunate but decent widow woman who unwittingly involved me in the whole strange business," he had written some fifty years later for that obscure Australian newspaper. "For I took pity on her and her grief for her lost sailor husband and one thing just led to another . . ."

It certainly had done, but not – naturally – exactly as the former junior officer of the Wavy Navy described it to his readers in far-off Oz.

They had agreed on a pound. It had been money well spent. She hadn't laid down off-putting ground rules as so many of the whores he had had dealings with usually did. He could touch her. He didn't need to wear a french letter. If he wanted to squeeze her breasts from underneath her bra it wouldn't be extra and, delight of delights, it'd only cost an extra half-crown to see her totally naked save for her black stockings and high heels in the freezing cold of the little flat to which she had taken him after the 'gin-and-it'.

It was then that she made the offer which, after some rapid mental arithmetic, he accepted hastily. If he agreed to feed the gas fire and paid her another 'two nicker' he could spend the night and have her as often as he wished. He jumped at the chance. It would be cheaper than going to one of the hotels near the station where they didn't ask too many questions, but where you still had to go through the silly rigmarole of pretending to be married, signing the register and giving the receptionist a ten-bob bribe.

She had only one condition. She wanted a little treat, if he were prepared to pay the half-crown each involved. "I mean," she said, pulling a fresh pair of black-market stockings on to her shapely legs, "it's what yer'd pay if you took me to the pictures, ain't it? Besides, Madame Clarissa's more spooky and exciting." She shivered. "She don't half put the wind up me, I can tell you."

He nodded, only half listening to her chat, concentrating on her near-naked body, warmed by the gas fire now hissing merrily at the foot of the bed. He'd put a full shilling in the meter to ensure that she remained naked as long as possible.

"When do you want to go?" he heard himself ask, gaze fixed hypnotically on the lovely breasts with their erect dark-coloured nipples. It was a hundred times better than any picture he'd ever fantasised over in *Health and Strength*.

"I thought we'd go and have some fish and taties in the cafe next to the fish shop at the corner. They're cheap and afterwards we'll go to her first séance at seven. She likes to start early. She doesn't want drunken matelots – you'd be surprised how many sailors from the fleet she gets – coming wandering in from the boozers causing trouble."

"Yes . . . damn nuisance, drunken sailors," he mumbled obediently, hardly aware what she was talking about.

It was only when she was nearly dressed and was dabbing *Soir de Paris* – "Comes straight from Paris," she boasted, though Paris had been in German hands ever since the summer – all over her upper body and behind her ears that he became aware of what she had been saying. "Séances," he said, looking at her quizzically. "Why do you go to séances, I mean, it's not like . . ." He let his voice trail away to nothing, unable to really put his thoughts into words.

She looked at him. For the first time her powdered, prettyish face revealed something about the real woman hidden by the professionally pleasing look of the street whore. "Because of my Bill . . ." She bit her bottom lip. "He went down with *Barham*, you remember?"

He nodded. Even de Vere's tiny middle-class prissy mind realised that he was witnessing some great emotion – one that he would never experience in his nice, tidy, orderly lifetime.

"She predicted the ship would go down, you know. She's very clever like that and a lot of us sailors' widows in Pompey, Plymouth and Poole and other places around here like to go to her now and again and see how our chaps are getting on—" she hesitated, as if she half wondered if he would laugh at the words she would use "—on *the other side*."

De Vere didn't laugh. Nor did he comment on the subject as they ate in the little cafe filled with the smoke of red-hot lard and the sharp odour of malt vinegar, listening to her babble on.

"Course, some people sez fish an' taties taste best out of paper, eatin' 'em with yer fingers. But I prefer 'em on a plate with knife and fork and best bread and butter . . ."

55

He wasn't really listening. His mind was still trying to deal with what she had said while she had been dabbing herself with the cheap scent, about the HMS *Barham*, that old Great War battleship that this 'Madame Clarissa', whoever she was, had predicted would 'go down'.

How would the old fake have known that? De Vere Smythe regarded all that business with Ouija boards, séances and 'voices from the other side' in the same light as reading tea leaves and gypsies looking into crystal balls: something for poorly educated working-class housewives and dotty old widows who were so senile they'd believe any damn thing.

But as they 'linked up', as Mavis called it, and set off for 'Madame Clarissa's Parlour', he kept his thoughts to himself. After all, when they got back and she got stuck into the half-bottle of Gordon's gin he'd bought under the counter from the knowing barman with a conspiratorial wink, he'd roger her again. There was no use upsetting her now, however stupid and silly her belief in the 'powers' of this fake medium was.

Lt Commander Ian Fleming of Naval Intelligence was in a foul mood. He'd gone with his chief, Vice-Admiral Godfrey, to meet 'C', otherwise known as Major-General Menzies, head of the MI6 organisation, at White's. He'd done his duty as a good staff officer should, and returned to the Admiralty to pick up the young Wren officer who, he'd confidently expected, would provide his night's sexual excitement for him, only to discover that some counter-jumper bounder of a civil servant had detailed her to drive him to see the PM at his country place at Chequers.

"Sorry, old boy," the airy answer to his angry query had come back over the scrambler phone in Godfrey's office, "hush-hush and all that, you know. Some sort of a flap at Chequers. Couldn't have sent anyone from the lower decks. Wouldn't have looked good and all that. Tootle-pip." And that had been that. The phone had gone dead.

But that had not been all. He'd been landed with the night watch in Room Thirty-Nine as well. He'd protested he'd done night duty only the previous week to no avail. The commander in charge, a regular, who had a down on Wavy Navy officers, had snapped with an air of finality, "This is not civvy street, Fleming. When you receive an order, you don't discuss it. You carry it out. If you have any complaints, you go through channels *afterwards*. Now carry on, Fleming, will you."

Fleming had 'carried on'. There was a flap on which concerned the Royal Navy and it seemed whatever he did, he couldn't find out anything about it. Twice he'd been up to the signal station on the roof of the Admiralty, with the flashes of the anti-aircraft guns ripping the night sky apart in slashes of angry scarlet, but the signallers had nothing to report. The Huns were raiding London, as usual – they had been doing so for the last four months – and tonight they were having a go at the south-western naval ports as well. But that was about it. Nothing of world-shaking importance as far as he could ascertain.

So the future creator of James Bond sat by the big marble fireplace, hugging the meagre flame – coal was running out again – polishing his well-manicured nails with his buffer and chain-smoking the gold-ringed cigarettes he had made specially in a shop off Bond Street, telling himself morosely at regular intervals that life was bloody shitty really – even considering it was wartime.

Thus engaged, he was startled by the sudden urgent ringing of the red-painted duty phone. It was the one that the Admiralty exchange had to give priority to and which members of Naval Intelligence only used in matters of urgency – save Fleming who often gave that number to his current 'popsy'. Hurriedly he reached for it, his bad mood forgotten immediately. Whatever it was, that phone always signalled excitement, beneath or outside the sheets.

A prissy voice answered which he could hardly recognise until the speaker gave his name – "Lieutenant de Vere Smythe here, sir" – and then he gave an inward groan at the information. It was that inferior middle-class twat of a former grammar-school teacher Smythe.

"Yes," he answered testily. "Where's the fire at this bloody time of the night?" For it was already approaching midnight and after twenty-three hundred hours, Room Thirty-Nine rarely got any more signals from Bletchley. Hitler's admirals, it seemed, went to bed with the chickens.

Smythe gave a faint chuckle. "Speaking of fires, sir, there really are some. We're being bombed again."

"Good for you, Lieutenant," Fleming said coldly, using the damned schoolteacher's rank to put him well and truly in his place. "Get on with it. I haven't all the time in the world, you know. We're busy here."

Sink the Hood

"Yes sir . . . sorry sir. I wouldn't have bothered you till morning, sir. But she's moving on, sir, and I really do think we should take action against her before she does any more damage. I—"

"For Chrissake, man," Fleming exploded, for he had a short fuse at the best of times and Smythe seemed to be suffering from verbal diarrhoea. "Get on with it, will you?"

"It's the woman . . . A kind of fake medium I just went to see some hour or so back. I didn't want to go because I can honestly say I think such people are crooks, right from the very start, sir. In addition—"

"Smythe!" Fleming cut him off, voice icy and full of upper-class menace.

Smythe understood. Fleming could hear him gasp audibly at the other end of the line before stuttering, "Sir . . . I think I've discovered a spy, my first in counter-intelligence – and a naval one."

"What in thunder do you mean, man?" Fleming snarled. He'd heard Smythe well enough, but the idea that the ex-grammar-school teacher of foreign languages could really have uncovered a spy was beyond belief. Why, the man couldn't find his way out of a bloody paper bag!

"Sir . . . a *German* spy. I'm sure of it." Hurriedly the junior officer filled Fleming in, while the latter's agile, inventive brain raced. He could see what the other man was getting at. There certainly seemed to be something funny about this Clarissa woman and the way she attracted gabby naval widows and dotty mums to her so-called séances. It was worth looking at it – and it would certainly be a feather in his cap if he could pull

59

something off down there in Plymouth. He knew he had plenty of enemies in the Admiralty, who thought of him as Admiral Godfrey's spoiled pet who was working a cushy number here in London. It'd be one in the ruddy eye for such folk if he really could unmask a genuine German agent.

"Listen, Smythe," he snapped urgently, as soon as the latter had finished his stuttered, excited explanation. "As soon as I can find the assistant watch-keeper, I'm getting a staff car and coming to see you. Do what you can to secure your end and see this Madam Clarissa, or whatever she's called, doesn't do a bunk. I want to speak to her. Get it?"

"Got it."

"Right, then do it." With that Fleming slammed the phone down hard. Ten minutes later he was gone, with the assistant watch-keeper still struggling into his clothes further down the corridor and the phone in Room Thirty-Nine ringing its merry head off – for reasons which wouldn't be explained till it was all too late . . .

Six

The shabby drifter passed the main fleet anchorage and started to run in between the islands of Fara and Flotta. On the bridge of the battered old craft, its single stack belching thick black smoke, the skipper eyed the bare purple hills of Hoy directly ahead. It was still the early hours of the morning, but in these northern climes dawn came early. Indeed, at this time of the year it never really seemed to get dark properly.

Next to him, Oberleutnant Hartung of the Regiment Brandenburg said in English – Canaris had ordered them to speak English as a precaution all the time, even when they were with their comrades from the special Secret Service regiment – "That's Lyness . . . to your front, sir." He indicated an untidy straggle of huts and oil tanks in the distance. Above it was the neat white cross of the naval cemetery.

"Yes, Hartung," the skipper, who spoke better English, answered. "The cemetery tells me. In there are buried the dead of the 1916 battle, English and our own people. Plus those of the High Sea Fleet who died after the—" "—business of 1918." The tough-looking commando officer completed the sentence for the naval officer. He knew that the navy people didn't like to talk about the surrender of the German High Sea Fleet to the victorious Tommies after the Great War.

The skipper nodded and concentrated on steering a straight course down the shipping lane, which was cleared of mines daily. All the same, his mind lay on the task ahead. To him it seemed almost a suicide mission, venturing like this into the heart of the enemy's greatest naval anchorage, Scapa Flow, trying to find out the information that the people in the *Tirpitzufer* 'God Box' – Canaris' headquarters – wanted, and then trying to make a run for it before the tea-drinking Tommies woke up to the fact that they had been caught with their knickers down.

Still, he told himself, they had an even chance of getting away with it. Their cover was good. The battered Norwegian drifter from Trondheim had been part of the enemy's 'Shetland Bus', which carried supplies and agents back and forth between the two countries, before the Secret Service had seized it, complete with codes, recognition signals and so on. It had got them this far without even being seriously challenged. But their luck wouldn't hold out for ever, he knew that. Recognition signals were changed regularly at odd intervals. At any rate, he'd have to be on his guard. Once the balloon went up, he'd do a bunk and shit on the fine gentlemen of the God Box.

They chugged ever closer to their objective. To starboard the skipper could now see the destroyer's anchorage. It was busy. There were destroyers there, plus a fleet auxiliary and what looked like a couple of coasters. That pleased the young, tough-looking German captain. His own craft wouldn't be too out of place, he told himself, in this massive naval anchorage.

He flung a fleeting glance to the north. There he could just make out the bottom of the German battle-cruiser *Derfflinger* of the scuttled Imperial German Fleet, which the Tommies had razed just before the outbreak of war. His face hardened. It reminded him of his duty to that old navy, stabbed in the back by the Jews and Reds back home in 1918. That kind of abject surrender would never happen again. German pride and achievement wouldn't allow it. Despite the danger of this daring mission, he felt a growing sense of purpose. He'd see the Brandenburgers through, come what may. He didn't know what the champagne pissers of the God Box in Berlin were up to. It didn't matter. The success of this mission did.

Time passed, but despite the slowness of the captured Norwegian craft and the monotony of that dreary landscape, the men on deck, both army and navy, were not lulled into a sense of false security. Indeed, the atmosphere was electric with restrained tension as the Brandenburgers waited for the orders to go into action. They all knew the danger they were in. Dressed in British Army uniform, they'd be shot out of hand if the Tommies captured them. But that didn't seem to worry the Brandenburgers particularly. Most of them had been through the same sort of thing, disguised as Polish, Belgian and Dutch soldiers in the invasions of those countries in the winter and spring of 1939–1940. Their concern was for the success of the mission. Although they didn't understand its aim fully, they had all been impressed by the little admiral's final words to them before they had flown off from Berlin-Tempelhof.

"Soldiers – comrades," Canaris had declared, his voice, for that secretive man, quite emotional for a few moments, "you have heard these words before, I know. *Germany's fate depends on the success of your mission* . . . But I salute you, Brandenburgers, for this time those words are true." With that he had touched his gloved hand to his battered cap and turned without another word, his shoulders bent, as if abruptly bowed with sudden emotion.

Now the gaze of the men on the bridge, which was open, attempted to penetrate the keen wind, which made their eyes water, and find the target. Here, with a bit of luck, they would find what their masters wanted of them and be back to the little Norwegian ship before the Tommies tumbled to the fact that anything untoward was happening. After all, why should the English expect any trouble inside this formidable naval base? It had been nearly two years since the submarine commander Prien had penetrated the anchorage with his U-boat and daringly sunk the British battleship the *Royal Oak*. Thereafter no other German vessel had attempted to do the same; it had been regarded as virtually impossible after that 'black Saturday', as the English had called it.

"*There.*" Hartung cut the tense silence of the bridge. He pointed. "Longhope!"

He was right. There was Longhope, five miles inside

the fiord that ran into Hoy, recognisable by the old-fashioned silhouette of the *Iron Duke*, the partly demilitarised warship with two of her turrets removed. They had arrived!

Now things happened fast. It had all been planned at Bergen two days before. The skipper and the engineer worked on the ancient engines. It wasn't very difficult. As the engineer exclaimed sourly, "Shit . . . shit . . . no decent German bumboat would tolerate an engine like this."

Within five minutes they had the machines clattering and panting, puffing out great clouds of evil black smoke as if they were on their last legs. Slowly the drifter started to slow to a halt and, in that same instant, the rubber dinghy containing the half-dozen Brandenburgers in British Home Guard uniform set off from the lee side, from which point they couldn't be seen from the little island hamlet, on their way to Longhope.

The mission was underway and while he posed on the open bridge, going through the motions of a very angry skipper for the benefit of any Tommy watching through a glass, the German captain started to count off the minutes. The next hour, before the watch boat would lift anchor and come to check what was going on with the shabby Norwegian craft, was to be vital. As he whispered out of the side of his mouth to the grumpy ancient engineer, as if the Tommies were already listening to them, "This is it, Heini – march or croak, eh?"

The latter's puffy face lit up in a craggy smile as he pulled out his flatman and offered the anxious skipper

65

a snort. "Well, sir, at least we can make a handsome corpse."

The skipper smiled wanly and accepted the bottle.

Hartung was careful but unconcerned now. Ice water seemed to be running through his veins. He told himself he'd been through it all before. In his mind he echoed the old engineer's phrase, '*marschieren oder krepieren*' – march or croak. If he was going to die, well, there it was. If he wasn't, well, good luck to him. He'd live – to die another day, as he surely would in the long war he suspected was to come. In the meantime he'd get drunk, feed his face with the best grub he could afford and undoubtedly get his ashes raked a couple of times by some whore or other.

Now he watched, eyes narrowed to slits against the icy wind, as the hamlet came closer and closer. He knew the place contained no civilians to speak of. The place was strictly naval – hence the Home Guard uniform, which might prevent the sailors asking too many awkward questions. Not that there'd be many of *them*, either. As the intelligence officer who had briefed them had declared, "Men, you'll find there are more seals sunbathing on the beaches of that arsehole of the world than human beings. They say the poor shits stationed there write love letters to the local sheep." The sally had raised a laugh, but not much of one. For the men had realised for the first time just how far from home they were being asked to go to carry out their dangerous mission. During all the other missions they had carried out in the last two years of total war, they had been able to walk home if things had gone wrong. Not on this one. It would be too far even to swim. Besides, the arctic temperature of those northern waters would probably kill them, if they attempted to do so, within minutes.

A quarter of an hour later the engine turned off and the dinghy ground to a halt in the soft sand of the inner bay. There was no sound save that of the curlews they had disturbed and, somewhere far off, the baaing of sheep like the cries of lost children. Hartung nodded and grasped the Browning Light machine gun of Great War vintage he was carrying – Intelligence thought it might have been the type the Americans had supplied to the Home Guard – and jumped into the knee-deep water. It was freezing. He repressed a gasp by an effort of will. Behind him the other five men did the same, while the corporal in charge of the smoke discharger, who would remain behind to cover the retreat if necessary, secured the rubber craft against the soft lap-lap of the icy wavelets.

Almost noiselessly they moved forward and breasted the sandy rise. Hartung flashed a look to left and right. Nothing moved. Over in the handful of rough, tumbledown shanties, smoke curled in a thin grey whirl from one of the stovepipe chimneys. Not even a dog barked. *If they have hounds in this arsehole of the world*, he told himself contemptuously and placed his hand, fingers splayed outwards, on the top of what he called his 'pisspot helmet', that of the English Home Guard. It was the infantry signal for 'advance'.

Dutifully his men followed him. Veterans that they were, they needed no orders. They spread out, crouched low, fingers on the triggers of their weapons, ready for anything. Hartung nodded his approval. They were good boys.

Metre by metre they crept forward. They passed the first of the shanties. He felt the wall in passing. It was ice-cold and not a sound came from the place. It was empty and had been so for long enough. That pleased him. Perhaps this was going to go off without trouble after all. He had told the young skipper of the drifter, "I have a feeling that the clock's in the pisspot and we'll be up to our hooters in shit once we get ashore, Oberleutnant."

Now, it seemed he had been wrong. Not even the clock had fallen into the pisspot so far. *Prima*!

They pushed on, starting to feel their way from cover to cover down a steep incline that led to their objective, the jetty where the lighters from the great ships, dim grey outlines in the far distance, were anchored in Scapa Flow. It was here that the little craft offloaded the men on leave and those going off sick and took on board fresh supplies for the crews on the water.

Many of the lighters were manned by half-naval and half-civilian crews, Hartung knew that from the Intelligence briefing, and all the storemen were civvies. So in the case of showdown, he didn't expect much trouble from the Tommies; most of them were probably unarmed. All the same, Intelligence had picked this ungodly hour for the reconnaissance because the big shots in the God Box assumed most of the Tommies would still be in their bunks for another hour at least.

Hartung hoped they were right, though the stomach-churning smell of frying bacon coming from one of the tin shanties next to the jetty told him that some, at least, of the Tommies were awake. He prayed that they'd be too busy frying that disgusting breakfast fodder of theirs – it wasn't natural to be scoffing fried food at this time of the morning – to take a look outside and spot the intruders.

Unfortunately for Hauptmann Hartung, his forecast was to be proved badly wrong.

Five minutes passed in tense, nervous excitement. Now they were on the jetty itself. Hartung gave a whispered order and the men straightened up. Now they looked, he hoped, like a Home Guard squad out on a boring early-morning routine patrol before they could return to their normal daily jobs. He felt this was the right way to attract as little attention as possible to themselves.

While his men took on the expressions of bored part-time soldiers killing time before they went off duty out of the freezing wind, Hartung's keen blue-eyed gaze took in the wooden uprights with the names of the ships placarded upon them as the spots where the ships' lighters would tie up ready to take on stores. To Hartung it seemed a gross lack of security. But then, he told himself, the Tommies obviously didn't expect any enemy to penetrate so far into the greatest naval base of their empire.

Moving his lips as he did so, Hartung read the names of the British ships, telling himself that if he were a real spy he'd be able now to assess the strength of the whole British Home Fleet from the neatly printed official signs giving the names of the ships the lighters supplied.

Suddenly, almost startlingly – although he had naturally expected to find it there; Intelligence had told him he should – there it was. These simple four letters of the great ship's name. He had found that she was there, virtually as easily as clicking his fingers.

"Grosse Kacke am Christbaum!" he cursed to himself with joy. "I've got it!"

For a brief moment he savoured his triumph, his hard-weathered face lighted up with joy. Then he became strictly professional once more, telling himself it was the fool who hesitated who got his balls caught up in the wringer. It was time to go while they were winning. He spun.

"Klemenz," he began, addressing the NCO closest to him, *"Los, hauen wir ab!"*

It was that same instant that a sharp angry challenge came from the door of the corrugated iron shed to their right; stabbed into their beings like the blade of a sharp knife. "Halt . . . who goes there?"

Hartung spun round.

An angry, helmeted face was staring at them. But it wasn't that which caught his attention. It was the long rifle with its old-fashioned bayonet which the sailor sentry was pointing in their direction which did.

Hartung reacted instinctively. He knew he had to. He brought up the silenced pistol which he had kept concealed all the while and fired low. The pistol jerked in his big fist. A puff of smoke, a soft plop and suddenly the sailor was going down, a look of total astonishment on his face, a red patch beginning to spread across the front of his greatcoat – and, in that last dying moment as he fought against falling to the ground and death, his forefinger, curled around the trigger of his Lee Enfield, jerked backwards.

The rifle exploded with what seemed to Hartung to be a tremendous crack of thunder. Then they were running back up the jetty to the hidden dinghy and rifle shots were ringing out on all sides, joined an instant later by the dreary dirge of the air raid sirens sounding the alert. They had been rumbled. Now it really was 'march or croak'.

Seven

The Spitfires had gone.

The drifter had proved too slow for them. At 300 miles an hour they had come zooming in at wave-top, machine guns chattering frantically – and had overshot the German craft by yards. Their slugs had lashed the grey-green water to a white fury quite without purpose. They had come in a couple of times more, while the skipper on the open bridge, sweating heavily despite the freezing cold, had dodged and zigzagged desperately. Then they had given up. Obviously their fuel had begun to give out and they had departed, disappearing into the ever-thickening cloud for their bases on the Scottish mainland.

For a while, the young skipper had hung limply at the wheel, his hands trembling helplessly. Hauptmann Hartung had said something from below, his hands red with blood, a shell dressing unwrapped and ready to apply to the wound of one of his men. But he hadn't been able to take in whatever the Brandenburg officer said. Besides, he was attempting to regain his nerve. The Tommies would be back. He knew that with the certainty of a vision.

The Brandenburgers had managed to get away, save one, Hartung had gasped as he had clambered over the side. He had been killed outright by a burst of machine gun fire. But that hadn't been the end of it. Indeed, within what had seemed only minutes all hell had been let loose. Everywhere sirens had begun to wail their dread warning. On the land, signal flares had shot alarmingly into grey sky. Signal lamps had blinked on and off between the great ships. Even anti-aircraft searchlights had been switched on over Flotta as if the Tommies thought they were being raided from the air.

But the young German skipper had been more concerned with the motor boat protecting one of the booms which had taken up the chase immediately. Going all out, a white bone in her teeth, curved prow standing right out of the water, she had narrowed the distance between herself and the civilian craft at an alarming speed. Even when she had been out of range, her quick-firer on the forward deck had started to spit flame. Tracer shells had zipped towards the German vessel in a lethal morse. Naturally they had fallen short, as the skipper had zigzagged desperately, great white spouts of whirling water erupting on both sides of her stern buffeting her from side to side, as if she had been punched by some gigantic invisible fist.

However, Intelligence had provided the bold intruders with some protection for such an eventuality as this sudden chase. The young skipper knew it was time to use the rough-and-ready device which the gentlemen of the God Box had provided. He snapped out of his battle-shocked reverie and shouted, "Obermaat – *jetzt los . . . DALLI, DALLI, MENSCH!*"

The grizzled old chief petty officer at the stern needed no urging. As he had told his mates in the petty officers' mess, "I don't fancy spending the shitting war scoffing English corned beef, drinking that shitting tea and playing the five-fingered widow in some Tommy cage, mates." The twenty-six-year-old skipper saw the danger quicker than the 'Old Man'.

With a grunt, he heaved the first of the tiny mines overboard. Immediately he followed it by another – and yet another. Suddenly the bubbling white wake of the drifter was filled with bobbing lethal metal eggs.

"For what we are now about to receive," the old salt gasped cheerfully as he shoved the last of the mines overboard, "may the Good Lord make us truly thankful." Then he waited.

He hadn't had long to do so. At the very last moment the skipper of the Tommy motor boat had spotted the deadly mines. Frantically he had swung his wheel to port. Too late! The sharp prow had struck the first of them in the fleeing drifter's wake. There was a thick throaty crump. The motor boat stopped abruptly, as if it had run into a brick wall. Next moment, its prow rose into the air in a ball of flame and a second later bits and pieces of man and metal were flying heavenwards. The happily brutalised Obermaat chuckled and crooned the old phrase, "Roll on death, mates, and let's have a fuck at the angels . . ."

That had been half an hour ago and with the suddenness of the northern climes, a thick white woolly fog had come rolling in and covered the Germans' flight, until the Spitfires had found a 'window' and come zooming down for their abortive strike. But now, as the almost exhausted skipper tried to concentrate on the course home to the safety of Bergen on the Norwegian coast, that window in the fog persisted. Indeed, it seemed to the harassed young officer that it followed the drifter as it headed eastwards. "For Chrissake," he hissed to himself angrily more than once, "will you bloody well go away."

But the window in the fog stubbornly refused to do his bidding.

In the distance, the big white bulk of a Sunderland flying boat from the Tommies' Coastal Command was coming ever closer, approaching with relentless determination. The old Obermaat spat out a stream of tobacco juice into the foam sea at the drifter's stern, crossed himself in mock solemnity and muttered to himself, "Heaven help a sailor on a shitty night like this." Then he thrust his skinny shoulder against the butt of the vessel's anti-aircraft gun. There was going to be trouble . . .

"Trouble; you can bet yer bottom dollar, Fleming, there's going to be trouble." Godfrey's irate voice crackled across the radio waves as the big staff Humber roared through the weak dawn light towards Plymouth and the waiting de Vere Smythe. There were silent flickering pink flames on the horizon to indicate the naval port had suffered yet another enemy coastal blitz. But Fleming, holding on with one hand behind the Wren and gripping the earphone tightly to his left ear with the other, had no eye for the fires. His whole being was concentrated on the surprising news that the Chief of Naval Intelligence was relaying from a still sleeping Chequers.

"The PM's gone to bed in a furious temper. He wants a report first thing in the morning when he wakes up. Northern Command is screaming bloody murder and my piles are playing me up like merry hell."

Under normal circumstances Fleming would have made one of his customary flippant remarks, especially about the piles. Now, however, the Lieutenant Commander thought it wiser to remain very professional and attentive. He said, "But what exactly happened at Scapa Flow, sir?"

"Nothing in one way," came back the surprising answer, but before Fleming had time to comment, Admiral Godfrey cried, "but on the other hand, all sorts of strange things did occur. The Hun landed there for one thing. Only one very small party, but they definitely came ashore. We found one of the cheeky buggers – only unfortunately, he'd been shot through the heart by some bloody Navy marksman. And I always thought matelots couldn't bloody well shoot straight."

"Anything?" Fleming cried above the furious squeal of rubber as the Wren driver took a corner far too fast, still whistling that damned jingle through her front teeth like a street-corner errand boy: "I've got spurs that jingle-jangle-jingle as I go riding merrily along . . ." Fleming would have dearly liked to have told her what to do with her spurs, but he thought better of it. She was in charge of the big car, after all.

"Anything that could give us a clue?" he repeated at the top of his voice, as the Wren took the car back up to seventy once more, whizzing down the blacked out village street.

"Just that the Jerry stiff was wearing a German tunic beneath the Home Guard blouse and it bore the Brandenburg armband on the right sleeve."

Fleming whistled softly. Now that really was something for the books, he told himself. Old Admiral Canaris' house troops.

Godfrey must have heard the whistle, for he shouted from the other end, "Yes, I know what you mean. Canaris wouldn't use his elite for anything in the nature of a common-or-garden commando raid. There's more to it than that."

"But what about the plane or ship which brought the Brandenburgers to Scapa Flow?" Fleming butted in, intrigued despite the Wren's crazy and highly dangerous style of driving.

"Ship, Ian," Godfrey answered. "Coastal Command's spotted it and one of their Sunderland flying boats is ready to go into the attack. But that's it. If the Hun craft gives the Sunderland the slip, we've had it. There's thick fog up there – too much for our surface ships. The Admiralty's not prepared to risk anything bigger than a torpedo boat, especially under present circumstances, until we can bloody well tell them what's going on. As if *we* damn well knew," Godfrey ended bitterly.

"Take your point, sir. But what do you want me to do? Should I continue to Plymouth or should I scrub the meeting with de Vere Smythe and hie myself tootsweet up to Scapa?"

"Not just yet. See what you can find out from that impossible counter-jumper Smythe. Report to me at zero eight hundred hours. Then I'll decide. Somehow" – Godfrey hesitated – "I have a funny feeling about this whole strange business . . ." He dropped his normally somewhat booming voice, acquired on the quarterdeck of the battle-cruiser he had commanded before 1939, and said, almost as if he were talking to himself, "There's a connection . . . I'm damn sure there's a connection."

"Between what, sir?" Fleming enquired, puzzled. He had always taken Godfrey for a straight character with no doubts: a plain-speaking sailor of the old school.

Godfrey didn't answer directly. Instead he said, "Continue with your present assignment, Ian, as I've said, and then we'll see." The connection went dead and as the big boxlike staff car raced on and on, Fleming sat for quite a while with the dead earphones of the wireless receiver in his hands, wondering what was going on and what the old Admiral had meant by saying that he was 'damn sure there was a connection'. A connection between *what*?

He could find no logical answer to that particular puzzling question and in the end he took a sip of the single malt whisky he always kept in his silver pocket flask, settled down more comfortably in the back seat and, closing his eyes, attempted to sleep till they reached Plymouth and the new problems that awaited him there.

Eight

"**E**r, well, sir, I'd say it was a pretty typical sort of a crowd that you'd find attending that kind of mumbo-jumbo. Mostly women" – de Vere Smythe never could refrain from expressing his middle-class snobbery – "of the lower orders, naturally."

Lower orders! Fleming, a snob of a different kind himself, groaned inwardly at the expression. But he said nothing aloud. Outside, the bombed city was settling down and a loudspeaker truck from Civil Defence was cruising by at a snail's pace, announcing, "Lists of casualties are now being posted at the Central Library . . . Those who have lost their homes should report this afternoon at the Guildhall for information . . . Ration cards which have been lost or destroyed will be replaced at . . ."

"A couple of middle-aged ladies, you know, sir, knitting and twin sets, and half a dozen matelots at the back looking a bit sheepish, as if they didn't really like being seen there. Not that they could be, really. Right from the very start, the lights were kept pretty dim. And it was nothing to do with the blackout. *He* obviously wanted to keep it that way."

"Who?"

"The organiser."

"What did he look like?"

"Big, surly-looking chap, about ten years younger than Madame Clarissa," de Vere answered, obviously enjoying the question-and-answer session – as if he thought himself doing a bloody Doctor Watson to my Sherlock Holmes, Fleming couldn't help telling himself sourly.

"Think he might be her boyfriend," de Vere continued. "That sort of thing."

"All right, when everyone had coughed up their entrance fee and had settled down, what happened next?" Fleming asked.

"Not much out of the ordinary, sir. The sort of thing you might have found at the WVS or the Mothers' Union. A lot of old – and young – biddies gossiping away about nothing. After a while, though – I hardly noticed it at first – there was music."

"Music?"

"Yes. Soft and mysterious somehow. I knew the tune, but for the life of me I can't remember the title of the piece now. Very soothing, though, almost soporific. I felt my eyelids blink a couple of times, I can tell you. I thought I was going to fall asleep." De Vere smiled faintly at the memory and told himself he'd had good reason for feeling tired – nay, exhausted would have been a better word. First there had been the session in Mavis' bedroom and then, lo and behold, in that crowded, hot, fetid atmosphere she had reached her naughty little fingers in underneath the greatcoat he'd folded over his lap – it had been so warm that he'd taken it off almost immediately – opened his flies and pulled his thing out of his pants. Nothing like that had happened to him before. A woman playing with his thing in a public place, utterly without shame. He had been so shocked – and, he had to admit it, tremendously excited, too – that he hadn't attempted to stop her.

So, while some silly old biddy next to him waffled on about how difficult it was to get offal these days, though it wasn't rationed, she'd been pulling at his thing for all she was worth and he could feel himself shaking and glowing with heat, knowing that in a minute, if she didn't stop that delightful torment, he'd be spraying all over her cunning dear hand.

"And?" Fleming demanded harshly, killing that delightful memory immediately.

"Oh, well, Madame Clarissa appeared from behind a curtain at the back of the room. The end of the place was lit by a dim red light so it was pretty difficult to make her out properly. But she was wearing a large robe – she's a large woman – that was a bit like a bell-tent."

"Was she wearing head covering too?" Fleming asked eagerly. "Also very loose?"

Smythe looked at his senior, surprised. "Yes. How did you know?"

Fleming indulged him. "Old trick with these dodgy mediums. The loose clothes can conceal things. They can also be got out of quickly and the medium can emerge wearing a totally different outfit for a while. In other words, the loose robe may hide a second person – from the other side." He emphasised the words cynically.

"Crikey!" Smythe was so awed that he reverted to the working-class slang of his youth: a fact that Fleming, the

81

old Etonian snob, noted immediately.

"Well, then the chap in charge said that Madame was going to go into a trance in the chair at the back on a kind of little stage – again, that red light made it difficult to see much – and that we were to keep quiet and say nothing until she was 'under'."

"I'd put her bloody well under," Fleming said grimly. "The damned traitor." By now he had made up his mind about Madame Clarissa.

Outside a middle-aged warden, the tears streaming down his honest, hard-working face, was carrying the body of a little child like some broken doll, exhibiting her to the silent crowd as he stumbled across the smoking brick rubble to the ambulance. Was he asking for someone to identify her? Or was he exhibiting her limp broken body like this, with her dangling little legs, as an expression of man's inhumanity to man? Fleming cursed beneath his breath. He was a cynical, uncaring man normally, concerned solely with his own personal pleasures and career. But this hurt. Someone had to be hurt in return – and it might as well be Madame Clarissa, if he could find the fat cow in time.

"Get on with it," he said urgently.

"It was a bit eerie, I must admit," Smythe continued. "She said something in a kind of gibberish, then she began swaying back and forth as if she were in the throes of a fit, all sorts of rubbish coming from her mouth. For a few moments I could have sworn she was cussing like a trooper – all sorts of vile words. Then suddenly, very suddenly – indeed, she gave me and the rest of the audience quite a start –

she stopped her writhing and trembling. She sat like that for what seemed an age. You could have heard a pin drop . . ."

It had been then that Mavis had stopped playing with his penis, so rigid by that stage that it hurt him physically. He would have dearly loved to have begged her to finish him off then and there, damn what people might think. But he didn't. The atmosphere in the tight, smelly room was like that of a church – a church in which the congregation was about to witness a miracle.

"It was then, sir – I know you might not believe this, but I *did* see it with my own eyes – that a sort of white cloud seemed to develop in front of Madame Clarissa. I know that the light was bad, but I saw it – and so did everybody else – and slowly, very slowly, the cloud began to form into what I can only call a rough-and-ready" – he paused and even now, hours after the event, he could feel the icy finger of fear trace its way slowly down the small of his back and make the hairs at the back of his head stand up – *"human figure."*

Fleming was unimpressed. Before the war he had been an avid reader of the thriller writer Denis Wheatley; he knew all about spiritualism and such things. "Ectoplasm," he announced, "probably a large, shaped bunch of cotton wool she'd hidden behind that robe you mention. It would have been the ideal hiding place for it. And then?"

"Once we'd got over the shock, she – or the, er, ecto-plasm; I couldn't really make out which – started talking. At first it was a lot of mumbo-jumbo. You know: *Uncle Joe is calling from the other side . . . Auntie May is feeling lonely . . . Is there anyone here tonight who'd like to reply?"*

"And of course there was," Fleming interjected.

"Yes; they were all a bit shocked or dazed, but once Madame Clarissa told 'em all was well they seemed pleased enough."

"Well, they got their money's worth. That's what they went there for in the first place."

"I suppose so, sir. But then it got even funnier – I mean, she did."

"How do you mean?"

"Well, she started speaking in a man's voice—"

"A man's voice?"

"Yes, sir. But that wasn't all. It was a tough, real down to earth sort of thing. You know, like the way that one of those old three stripeys of the lower deck talk – one of those who never acknowledges that he's in the company of women and talks like he does in his division – all 'bloody' and 'bastid' – and even worse, if you'll forgive my French." Smythe was plainly embarrassed. He even went red.

Fleming didn't seem to notice. He leaned forward and rapped urgently, "You mean like a matelot?" Before Smythe could answer, he followed with a swift "And what sort of questions did this – er – man ask?"

"You know that too, sir," Smythe said, surprised, then he saw the look in his superior's eyes and continued with a hasty, "Well, sir, leading questions, I'd call 'em."

"How leading?"

"For instance, he asked a stoker what his ship was – just like that. Then to top it all, he asked him whether he was bunkered up, meaning—"

84

"Meaning, he'd – er – she'd know whether his ship was about to sail!"

"That's what I thought, too." He was going to say more, but he could see from the look on Fleming's broken-nosed face that he was thinking hard and didn't want to be disturbed.

Outside the sweepers had arrived from the council, looking very like Royal Marines in the tall pith helmets they wore. They engaged themselves in sweeping away the broken glass and brick rubble. The city was being patched up and restored to normal until the next raid came – and it would come, Smythe knew that. They always did. Hun air raids had become part and parcel of everyday living in Britain these days. There seemed no end to them.

Finally Fleming broke his heavy brooding silence. "All right; I think we can assume that she is a spy. It is imperative that we arrest her. There's something very funny going on at Scapa, which I'll tell you about later. It might well be that this Madame Clarissa of yours has something to do with the events up there. The best way to find out is to grill her. Where is she, Lieutenant Smythe?"

Smythe looked miserable. He hung his head like a shamed schoolboy. "When the sirens sounded, sir, the air warden came in shrilling his whistle, crying 'everybody into the shelters'. You know how ruddy officious they can be – and there wasn't even a shelter, anyway . . . Before I could do anything, sir, the whole lot of them had disappeared. Later I checked her hotel."

"Yes?"

"She'd gone – and left no forwarding address. Why should she? After all . . ." The explanation died on his lips. He could see that Lieutenant-Commander Fleming wasn't listening. Besides, he could feel a strange burning sensation in his penis. He had experienced it an hour or so before when he had gone to the latrine to pee. Idly he wondered what it was.

"It's obvious she's on no theatre or music hall circuit now," Fleming said slowly and softly, as if musing to himself. "That might be too dangerous. If she had a fixed timetable she could be picked up at any time. All the same, she's travelling. But where?"

"Sir." Smythe cleared his throat and half held up his hand like a timid schoolboy asking some frightening beak, armed with a cane and quick to use it, if he might be excused.

After some time, Fleming deigned to notice him. "Yes?" he snapped impatiently.

"If I may be so bold, sir—"

"You may." But irony was wasted on Smythe.

"This Madame Clarissa . . . she works with sailors."

"So?"

"Well, the place where she'll find sailors is a port – a big naval port. As we know, she's been to Pompey and now Plymouth—"

"She'd never be able to get to Scapa," Fleming snapped, seeing the way that the other man was going. "It's out of bounds for civvies."

"I know, sir, but there are other naval bases which feed drafts and the like to Scapa for the Home Fleet up there. If she wanted to find out about our ships up there, she'd go to one of those places to pump the matelots for info."

"Of course," Fleming cried excitedly. His voice dropped. "But why did you think it was that place – and the ships up there – that this Madame Clarissa of yours is interested in, Smythe?" He stared hard at the other officer's weak pale face.

"That place?"

"Scapa Flow, Smythe," Fleming snapped.

Smythe's mouth dropped open with surprise. "I say, sir," he managed to gasp, his face suddenly frightened, his mind racing at the realisation he had just come to. "It must be catching, sir."

"What?"

"This seeing in the future stuff . . ." He looked earnestly at his superior's arrogant face. "Do . . . d'yer think I'm *psychic*, sir?"

Harding Waxes Poetic

I was bloody stymied!

Again I seemed to have come to a dead end in this half-century-old business of the *Hood*. Mr *sodding* de Vere Smythe had turned out to be a loser. He had whetted my appetite but when it came down to cases, he hadn't produced the grub. Perhaps they're all like that in Oz. It's all that sitting in the sun on the beach in funny hats drinking their disgusting 'bevvies'.

He had finished the letter accompanying 'my piece' from the bloody provincial Aussie rag with, 'I'm afraid I couldn't pursue the matter any further at the time. Lt Commander Fleming, who, as you know, departed for the other side' – God, he was beginning to start to sound like a bloody table-rapper himself – 'a long time ago now, did instigate a search for the missing Madame Clarissa, but as to whatever he may or may not have discovered then . . .'

I breathed out with exasperation. Didn't the little creep waffle! *He'd* never get a contract for a book from my publisher, that well-known patron of the Gay Hussar, I can tell you. He'd never be able to afford a book of the length that de Vere Smythe would produce. At a penny a word, it would bankrupt him. And that would be the end of crawling waiters, *paprika gulyas* and bottles of the finest Tokay. It'd be McDonald's after that . . .

'You see,' my correspondent had gone on, 'I was taken quite ill at the time from some sort of abdominal complaint. They shipped me straight off to the Haslar' – he meant the great wartime hospital at Portsmouth – 'and I never heard about the end of the affair with Madame Clarissa. It was, after all, very hush-hush . . .'

The words blurred. I looked out of the cottage window and I frowned at the cold remorseless North Sea and the drizzle. I remembered the burning sensation he'd mentioned and hoped that Mavis, that obliging lady of the night, had given him a nice juicy dose of the clap as a souvenir. It couldn't have happened to a nicer guy.

I smiled at my blurred reflection in the steamed-over window pane. In those days they didn't prescribe penicillin as a cure for the clap. So probably de Vere Smythe had had to suffer quite a while in the Haslar with his 'social disease', as they called VD in those far-off days.

My smile vanished and I frowned at myself. De Vere Smythe's troubles with sex and its after-effects didn't help me one bit. As for Fleming, he was not only dead, but the information he *had* left behind regarding his wartime Intelligence work was totally unreliable. How the hell did he get away with it? He travelled everywhere, rode the gravy train first class and as far as I could see never produced one solid contribution to British victory in World War Two during his whole six-year naval career. But then, look at the success of 007, as played by a former Scottish milkman, and an easy-going chap with warts who went to my old Catholic school in Leeds . . .

I digress. None of this took me one iota closer to what really happened to the *Hood*. How was I now going to get rid of that image of the old lady in her husband's boots running shrieking down that passage so long ago: 'The *Hood* . . . my son . . .'

Even now I can wake up sweating, heart beating like a bloody trip-hammer, hands trembling – and it's not the booze – when I recall that childhood memory. *She* deserves an explanation, if nothing else.

Outside the rain was beating a murderous tattoo at the window. I pretended I didn't notice. I had to concentrate. What did I know? *Bugger all, matey*, a coarse voice from the past sneered at the back of my mind. I ignored the voice and concentrated even harder.

I knew the facts – and damn few they were, too. The MOD wasn't coming across. Kew wasn't releasing the relevant documents. OK, that meant the Admiralty – and, naturally, the Government – had something to hide. What? How was it that the *Hood*, once the greatest ship in the world, was sunk so quickly? A matter of five minutes and she was gone, taking nearly two thousand poor souls with her. Such things happen in warfare, happen all the time – but not with such apparent ease. So what was so special about the way HMS *Hood* was sunk by the Germans in 1941?

A lot of questions and so few answers . . .

I must have sat there for quite a long time, pondering the ancient mystery. And wasted time means lost money for an underpaid hack writer.

In my type of book I rarely get a chance to quote the Bard. But he is handy. He's got a quote for everything and he's easier to remember than the Bible. What had he said about time? 'I wasted Time – and now doth Time waste me', or something of the sort. Exactly.

The quotation put the old brain into third gear. (These days it'd never make fourth without the gearbox blowing up.)

Who knows everything, can find out everything in the late nineties? Who's smarter and more efficient than the CIA – MI6 – MI5 – Bundesverfassungschutz, et cetera, et cetera, all bundled into one? Why, the British Press of course. With those magnificent cheque books of theirs, they can open virtually any door with a neat signature – at the bottom of a suitably large amount of the readies, of course. Those fools who govern us keep getting caught with their knickers down about their ankles because they haven't reckoned with that yet; they still think we live in the time of Queen Victoria.

So who did I know in the gutter press who could point me in the right direction? I mean, most tabloid hacks, as bright as they are, don't even know what they had for breakfast, liquid or otherwise, the previous day.

Then I had it. *Horace the Obit.* Horace would know – and if he didn't, he'd bloody well tell me where to find out.

I reached out for the black book and the phone and prepared for a long siege at the door of British Telecom. For a change I was happy, the woman in the boots temporarily forgotten . . .

Nine

Admiral Lutjens and Captain Lindemann were arguing. Even through the steel walls of Lindemann's cabin, Oberfahnrich Klaus von Kadowitz could hear them, as he waited next to the immaculate Marine sentry, together with Obermaat Hansen. He frowned. He didn't like to hear senior officers raising their voices, especially when there were men from the lower decks present. It wasn't good for morale, and he guessed that within the hour, the buzz about the two big cheeses being engaged in a slanging match would be doing the rounds of the *Prinz Eugen*. He looked at Hansen, but his rough, ruddy, drunkard's face revealed nothing, save perhaps a little look of joy at the cadet officer's discomfort. Instinctively, Klaus touched the new black enamel of the Wound Medal which decorated his chest now. It did show he had seen some action – even if it was only in an air raid – and had shed his blood for the Fatherland.

"I don't like it, Herr Admiral . . . I don't like it one little bit," he could hear the skipper Lindemann saying. Even the typical sound of the great ship, the low regular whirr and hum of the auxiliary machinery, couldn't drown their voices. Lutjens' reply, however, remained inaudible. Klaus's frown deepened. What in three devils' names could the Fleet's two most senior officers be arguing about? They commanded the most powerful ships in the world. Admittedly the Tommies outnumbered them collectively, but individually they were more than a match for anything the enemy could put in the field.

"We can safely assume that the Tommies will spot the *Bismarck*'s entry into the conflict in the North Atlantic once we reach Norway. As you know, we'll sail from Bergen with a fake convoy. Thereafter our two ships, *Bismarck* and *Eugen*, will break away for the action to come."

Lindemann nodded. His face revealed nothing of his doubts, only his resentment. It expressed his feeling that he was not able to represent his own doubts fully enough. He knew Lutjens didn't like Raeder's plans any more than he did. But Lutjens was out for glory; he'd carry out the plan in the knowledge that the Führer would reward him for doing so. Hitler always liked his commanders to barrel ahead without asking awkward questions.

"Now we must understand this," Lutjens continued quite severely, ignoring the look on the captain's face. "We can be sure that the Tommies are fully informed of our firepower and range of action, especially that of the *Bismarck*, our flagship."

Lindemann nodded, but said nothing.

"So they will throw in everything they've got, including the *Hood*, as Canaris has informed us. Well –" he hesitated, as if even he was not quite sure of himself and the outcome of the battle to come, – "come what may we must return with a victory or –" he hesitated again momentarily – "not at all."

Lindemann had expected the comment. He didn't like it. He had never liked, in all his career, these black-and-white statements of the more unthinking naval officers. Their rigid logic lacked finesse, and he had already prepared his counter-argument. "Herr Admiral, with your permission, I don't think we should look at the matter quite like that. There are not just two alternatives."

Lutjens gave him a sharp look. Outside he could make out the rumble of the tugs as they prepared to tow the *Prinz Eugen* out into the channel. He'd have to be leaving soon. "Pray continue," he said coldly.

"A victory we must have – to please the Führer. But let it be a limited one, and not one that is foolhardy and risks our two capital ships. As you know, Admiral, we're aiming at the *Hood*. Fine. We sink her and we have our great victory. Thereafter we make a run for it."

"I don't like that phrase."

Lindemann ignored the comment. If Lutjens wanted to be a hero, so be it. But he personally had no ambitions in that direction, especially if the glory was going to come posthumously. "In my opinion," he said quickly, as the first of the tugs nudged the side of the *Prinz Eugen* and sent the glasses on the tray shaking, "we can have our victory *and* save our ships from damage and possible destruction, if we're quick enough. In and out before the Tommies can gather their whole fleet and set about blasting our craft out of the water. After all, Herr Admiral," he reminded a stony-faced Lutjens, "the *Hood* will probably be the first on the scene, with her speed. She can outspeed the rest of the English fleet by at least eight or nine knots."

Lutjens humoured the red-faced captain with a nod. "I see . . . and?"

"And this. We keep this business secret as long as possible. Why should the English know that we're in Bergen? Why shouldn't they find out where we are much later, when their aircraft patrols finally pick us up? Then they'll send the *Hood* at top speed to intercept us." He paused for his punchline. "We'll have her on our own, Herr Admiral, and she won't have a chance in hell – not with our combined firepower."

Lutjens considered and then reached for his cap, as if he couldn't believe that his subordinate could do anything about the situation as it stood – after all, it had been planned at the very top, at the *Tirpitzufer*. He snapped gruffly, "And how, *mein lieber* Lindemann, will you ensure that we keep this business a secret 'as long as possible', as you phrase it? After all, we are sailing through one of the most busy of inland waterways, the Baltic."

Lindemann was ready for the question. "As you know, Admiral, the neutral Swedes have been warned to run for port now. They can guess what is going on, but they won't know. But there will be some of their skippers, the ones with the little boats that do all the contraband running between Sweden, Lübeck, Wismar and the like, who'll stay out in the Baltic. Anything they pick up, they'll sell to the Tommies' agents in Stockholm. They, Herr Admiral, will be the ones, if we allow them to do so, who pass on the information about the *Bismarck* and the *Prinz Eugen*. They are the ones, too, that we will – er – eradicate if necessary."

Lutjens looked at the *Eugen*'s skipper as if he had just cursed the Führer himself. "*Eradicate?*" He caught himself in time. He slapped his cap on to his shaven head and rose to his feet. "Do as you wish, Captain Lindemann. I for one don't want to know."

Lindemann stood to attention. Lutjens pressed his hand, seeing through his subordinate as if he were made of glass. "I shall see you in Bergen, Lindemann." Without another word he passed from the cabin and through the waiting sailors, all standing stiffly to attention in the companionway, staring at some distant horizon known only to themselves.

Hansen wrinkled his nose as if he had just smelled an unpleasant odour and Klaus von Kadowitz, loyal as he was, understood why the sailors called the Admiral '*der schwarze Teufel*' behind his back. He had no heart for his men. He would sent them all to hell without a moment's hesitation.

A minute later, the duty officer called them in and Captain Lindemann began to explain to Klaus and Obermaat Hansen what he wanted from them. Without ever being aware of it, the young officer-cadet, the hard-bitten petty officer and the score of young sailors under their command had become part of the greatest security and counter-intelligence operation ever prepared by Admiral Canaris.

* * *

Operation Bismarck, as it was code-named, had been planned with unparalleled thoroughness. Involving naval, army and counter-intelligence units, it began on that evening of May nineteenth from the Baltic through Bergen right up to the Artic Circle.

Infantry units were shipped in regimental strength to Bergen. Fake convoys sailed to and fro up the Norwegian coast. Minesweeping flotillas were everywhere, apparently sweeping areas where there hadn't seen a mine since the outbreak of war nearly two years before. Infantry and naval marines moved right up to Norway's remote border with Russia.

In Oslo, Canaris' counter-intelligence agents let the Norwegian spies signal what was going on in their area, though even the Norwegians couldn't make head nor tail of all this hectic activity. The Abwehr would pounce on the Norwegians on the morrow and close down their networks. Thereafter there would be total silence from Norway, presumably leaving the English more confused about what was going on than ever.

But still there was that problem of the inner sea, the Baltic. Here there was no hope of confusing the enemy, Canaris knew that. It was for that reason that he had suggested to the *Prinz Eugen*'s skipper, rather than to the Fleet Commander, Lutjens, that he should, as he had put it in that delicate manner of his, 'take special measures . . . even if they could be messy'.

The *Prinz Eugen*'s skipper knew, as did Hansen and even a reluctant Klaus, what that 'messy' meant. In his own inimical fashion, the old salt laid it on the line. "We croak 'em, Oberfahnrich. No two ways about it. If we suspect the Swedish saucehounds, it's a quick knock on the back of the turnip" – he meant skull – "and heave-ho, m'hearties – over the frigging side!"

They were sitting in the little bridge of the armoured motor boat which had been allotted to them for their task in the Baltic, watching the tugs pull the majestic bulk of the *Bismarck* through the evening mist so that it appeared like a ghost ship sliding mysteriously and silently on its mission of death. "Fine ship," Klaus said almost dreamily as he sipped his scalding hot coffee.

"Ay, that she is," Hansen agreed, his red swollen nose savouring the delightful odour of real bean coffee well laced with a hundred millilitres of strong rum. "You know, Oberfahnrich, I saw the Grand High Fleet sail out of Kiel to meet the Tommies at what they call the Battle of Jutland back in 1916. Snotty-nosed kid of fifteen at the time. Grand sight they were with the bands playing, the flags flying and even them bloody red dockies cheering 'em; social democrat to the man they were, too. And then . . ." He shrugged and stopped.

Klaus waited and, when nothing came, asked a little uncertainly, "And what then, Chiefie?"

"Not so many of 'em came back – and what did, didn't look so grand any more. We never left harbour again after that until the Tommies ordered us to sail to the surrender at Scapa Flow."

Klaus forced a grin. "A real ray of sunshine you are, Obermaat. That won't happen to us, I can tell you. We won't let it. After all, Chiefie, we have the finest, strongest and most modern ships in the world, you know." His chest swelled with pride. "This is a different Germany from the days when you were a kid. The whole nation's behind us now, Chiefie."

Obermaat Hansen was not convinced. Abruptly his good mood vanished.

With the enthusiasm and one hundred per cent confidence of youth, Klaus tried to reassure the dubious old salt. "Look at her." He indicated the *Bismarck* slowly disappearing into the mist. "She's all of forty-five thousand tons displacement. She carries eighty-nine guns of all calibres, her big guns sighted and aimed within a metre by radar – a helluva lot faster than those of the Tommies. As far as her armour is concerned, she has a nickel-chrome-steel torpedo belt right round her hull." He smiled confidently at the surly petty officer. "Hansen, you know and I know that there isn't a torpedo in the world powerful enough to smash through that torpedo belt. Hell, man, she's virtually unsinkable."

Hansen didn't reply. He continued to sip his coffee and rum, saying nothing, lost, it seemed, in his own thoughts – and they weren't pleasant.

Oberfahnrich Klaus von Kadowitz gave up on him. He sighed and said, "All right, Obermaat, I'm going below. You take over the con till we're out into the Baltic. *Klar?*"

"*Klar*, Herr Oberfahnrich." Hansen came to an approximation of attention, mug held at his side.

Klaus touched his fingers to his cap, battered in the approved fashion by dint of much hard work in the secrecy of his tiny cabin so that it would lend him the look of a veteran. He clattered down the companionway to go below deck. But before he did so, he flashed a final look upwards.

Hansen had put his mug down and was holding the wheel now. But Klaus could see he wasn't paying too much attention to the con. His eyes were fixed on some further point than the area immediately in front of him, in the wake of the tugs and the *Bismarck*. It was as if he were looking into another – and not so rosy – world, known only to him.

Idly Klaus wondered what it could be. Hansen, he told himself, didn't look the type given to introspection. Then he shook his head as if physically dismissing the matter and opened the door into the tiny wardroom and its thick fug, his mind already racing excitedly at the prospect of the great adventure to come.

Ten

A t first light, the fog came drifting in from the land. At first it was nothing more than a few faint grey wisps. They curled themselves like a soft silent cat around the motor launch, almost unnoticed.

On the deck the handful of young ratings went about their early morning duties without seeing it, emptying the slops from the night, throwing overboard the waste from the tiny galley, checking the 20mm Bofors mounted on the forward deck and the twin Spandaus behind the little bridge.

But slowly the mist thickened. It brought with it a freezing, bone-chilling cold, more intensive than normal for the Baltic in early spring. When it was time for the on-duty watch to do their morning 'physical jerks', they did so in their heavy sea-going gear and hobnailed winter boots and at the end a couple of the usual comics found on board every ship waltzed together in mock solemnity, stomping on the metal deck. But as the cold grew more intense, even the young men's high spirits deserted them and they went about their duties in an almost sullen, brooding lethargy. As Hansen grumbled to Klaus von Kadowitz, "It'll frigging well snow next, you just watch,

Oberfahnrich, you just watch!" And he was right. Half an hour later, as the last smudge of what had once been the Danish island of Rugen disappeared on the horizon, the first gentle flakes of snow came drifting down.

On the bridge, Klaus cursed. This was his first independent command and an important one at that. Now the fog and the lightly falling snow could only make his task more difficult. The Swedes running contraband in and out of the German Baltic ports would know this coast like the back of their hands; they'd know where to hide even under ordinary conditions. Now the weather conditions would make it even more difficult for a novice like himself to spot them.

At his side Hansen broke his silence and said, as if he could read the young skipper's mind, "Not to worry, Oberfahnrich. Those *Svenskas* are greedy swine. They're after our money and they're after the Tommies' cash. Neutral, my arse!" He spat contemptuously on the floor of the bridge, a habit which Klaus thought wouldn't be too well regarded in the higher circles of the German Kriegsmarine. "They're in this shitting business only for this." He made the gesture of counting money with his forefinger and thumb. "So, bad weather or not, they'll stay out at sea as long as they can without running for the shelter of the land. If we can stay out, them Swedish slime-shitters will, too. If it's gonna pay them to spot the *Bismarck* and our *Prinz Eugen*, they'll stay out, believe you me, Oberfahnrich . . ."

It was about noon, just after the off-duty watch had consumed their usual thick pea-soup and 'dead men's toes', otherwise known as sausages, that the lookout on the prow, tied into his little circle of steel railing to protect against being washed overboard, cried, "Object . . . port bow, sir!"

The sharp announcement broke into Klaus's reverie as he smoked somewhat moodily on the bridge, watching the fog roll in, wet, sad and sound-deadening. He stared at the lookout, muffled in his leather Joppe and thick fur hat, peering through his glasses trying to penetrate the grey fluffy damp gloom. "Where?" he called.

"Green one-zero, sir." The lookout amplified his original announcement.

Klaus von Kadowitz turned into the direction of the bearing and focused his glasses. Next to him Hansen waited, but said nothing. For what seemed a long time he saw nothing, then slowly and silently, almost in a sinister fashion, a clumsy, lumbering shape crept into the twin glittering circles of calibrated glass and, for an instant, he caught a fleeting glimpse of a blue and yellow flag painted on the slow craft's rusting side.

Hansen followed his gaze. "Got a nice big neutral flag painted on her side, has she?" he asked, drinker's voice full of cynical contempt.

"Well, she's a Swede – that's for sure."

"And what's one of those Swedish slime-shitters doing in the middle of nowhere, hove-to in weather like this, instead of going about her business of making green moss?" He meant money.

Klaus knew what the cynical petty officer – who smelled strongly of hard booze once more, as he usually did at regular intervals during the working day when he allowed himself 'one behind the collar stud', as he

103

phrased it – meant. The Swedes must have spotted the *Bismarck*. Now they were waiting for the great ship's escort to follow. That meant they were waiting for the *Prinz Eugen* and the destroyers. He didn't need a crystal ball to realise that he was in the presence of the Swedes – who were selling info to the Tommies.

Hansen read his thoughts. "It's them, isn't it, Oberfahnrich?"

"Yes," Klaus agreed slowly, as the frightening realisation started to dawn upon him that if he was right, he was going to have to do something about it.

The skipper had made his instructions quite clear. "If you find them, von Kadowitz," he had rasped, his thin-lipped mouth worked as if by rusty tight steel springs, "you must not hesitate. It will have to be a *Nacht und Nebel* action. Is that clear? There are to be no tell-tale survivors."

Nacht und Nebel. The customary police phrase now rang through the innermost recesses of his brain alarmingly, echoing and re-echoing as if it would never end. 'Night and Fog' – a puzzling phrase for a very simple – and very *final* – operation.

"Well, sir?" Hansen asked easily, as the young skipper lowered his glasses, face crestfallen at the knowledge of what he must soon do. "When do we begin to tango?"

Obviously there was no doubt in the petty officer's mind, either about the ship in the fog off their bow or what would soon have to be done with it. For him the matter was already decided.

"Do you think we ought to give them a chance?"

Klaus commenced, but the look on Hansen's tough, drunkard's face told him he was wasting his time.

"They wouldn't give us a frigging chance in hell. They'd sell us down the river, Oberfahnrich, in zero-comma-nothing seconds!" he said roughly.

Klaus bit his bottom lip, plagued with doubts. He knew what the skipper would want him to do. He knew, too, that Hansen had no doubts whatsoever about the course he must now take. Yet still he was not certain. He had never attempted to kill anyone, even though he had been in the service since he had volunteered straight from high school in 1940, as soon as he had been old enough to apply for an officer's commission. All the same, to decide to kill someone in this cold-blooded, clinical fashion when not a single shot had been fired at him was hard, very hard.

Hansen realised Klaus's indecision, for he spoke, breaking the sudden heavy silence, his voice not so gruff as it was usually. "Don't take on, sir," he said. "It happens to all of us once . . . the first time. But it's got to be done and when you've done it once, you go on doing it." He hesitated and, for an instant, Klaus could sense the old salt's inner warmth and humanity beneath that normal exterior of swaggering boozer's toughness. "It's almost like a habit . . . you don't even seem to be doing it. In the end it's just something you do because you're told to. It—" He broke off abruptly as if he had realised he had said enough already. Now the decision was up to the tall handsome aristocratic officer-cadet facing him, his gaze worried and anxious.

"You're telling me," Klaus von Kadowitz said after a moment, the only sound the steady throb of the motor boat's engine at slow speed, "to use your own pretty phrase, Hansen, it's either piss or get off the pot?" He forced a tight-lipped smile.

"Something like that, sir."

"*Gemeinnutz vor Eigennutz*," Klaus muttered as if to himself.

Hansen waited, saying nothing, his eyes fixed once more on the dark object bobbing up and down on the horizon, unsuspecting and trapped already, though her crew did not yet know it.

"All right." Klaus made his decision. "*Beide Motoren voraus . . .* half speed. We don't want to alert the Swedes just yet."

"*Beide Motoren voraus.*" Hansen almost whispered the young skipper's instruction down to the waiting engine-room artificer below.

Almost instantly the two powerful engines throbbed into half power. It was like a highly strung thoroughbred being released from the trap. The motor boat's prow rose from the water. A small white bone appeared at her sharp knifelike bow. She surged forward, gathering speed at every monent. Automatically Klaus grabbed a stanchion to prevent himself from being knocked over against the side of the tiny bridge.

Hansen handed over the con to Klaus. "If it's all right with you, sir, I'll take care of the peashooter." He meant the 20mm and Klaus knew instinctively why he had made the offer. He was volunteering to take over the dirty work of opening fire on the unsuspecting Swedes.

He forced a grin, though he had never felt less like

106

smiling in the whole of his young life. "You've got a heart of gold, Obermaat."

"And an arse full of piles," the latter answered somewhat obscurely. Then he was gone and Klaus was left alone with his thoughts. They were not, it must be said, very happy ones . . .

Two hundred miles away at the other side of the Baltic, the middle-aged Royal Navy captain masquerading as a British naval attaché waited impatiently down in the bowels of the cellar which housed the British Legation's secret radio station.

Despite his outward calm, the middle-aged professional sailor, now turned temporary diplomat, was nervous, even a little flustered. Time and time again he looked at the well-shaven neck of Sparks, the naval rating who acted as his secret signaller, as if anticipating that he might spring into action at any moment. But each time he was disappointed. Grumpily he eased his ring round his tight starched white collar. Dammit, he was beginning to sweat now. At this rate, with this damned Swedish super steam heat – the Swedes did love to spoil themselves, considering they were supposedly the descendants of the hardy Vikings – he'd be stinking like a pig by lunchtime.

For days now Captain Denham of Naval Intelligence had known there was some kind of flap going on at the other side of the Baltic in Nazi Germany. He had been too long at this funny sort of war-in-the-shadows not to be able to smell a flap when there was one. It was the same at the nearby German Legation in Stockholm. The Hun diplomats had refused all invitations for the last week or so and had virtually disappeared from the capital's social scene. He could guess why. They'd been ordered to do so from Berlin. All the same, he hadn't the foggiest what the bloody flap was about.

Still, he had guessed it would come within the area covered by the office of the naval attaché. One clue to that fact was that the pro-German Swedish naval intelligence service was watching him once more. As he had remarked the night before to his opposite number in the army, "Carruthers, dammit all, I found one of the Swede buggers trailing me into the gents at the International Club this lunchtime. I mean, people will begin to talk." The military attaché had guffawed in that horselike manner of his – indeed, he did look a bit like a clapped-out cavalry mount – and Denham had joined in. But in reality it had been no laughing matter. Swedish Intelligence didn't trail diplomats unless they were worried what the latter might find out.

But what could they be worrying about? Captain Denham pursed his lips, which were dry for some reason – perhaps it was the general mood of nervousness at the Embassy – and considered the matter. Naturally, the less the British knew about Swedish shipments of ball bearings and other strategic materials to the Huns, the better pleased the Swedes were. The same applied regarding the case of the neutral Swedes allowing the Germans to use their railway networks to transport the vital iron ore from Occupied Norway to the ice-free Swedish Baltic ports to the Reich.

Yet somehow, sweating it out in that hot underground

cellar, Captain Denham thought what was happening now had nothing to do with the supply of material for the German war machine. It was something else, something more directly connected with the conduct of the war.

Now, as he waited, he prayed and hoped that his tame Swedish contraband runners out in the Baltic off the German coast, palms well greased with British gold, might provide him with an answer to his problems.

He was just considering whether he should light another cigarette from the glowing stub of the one that he had about finished when the back of the radio operator's neck stiffened. He forgot the cigarette instantly. "Got something, Sparks?" he barked urgently.

Instead of answering, the smart young radioman fiddled with his dials with one hand, clapping his earphones closer to his ears with the other as if he were finding the reception difficult.

Denham swallowed hard. He leaned forward tensely. This was it, he told himself. He waited, fighting back his almost overwhelming desire to question the radio operator, who was now scribbling down figures urgently with his left hand, while adjusting the controls of his receiver with his right – a skilled trick that only very experienced 'sparks' could manage.

Finally Captain Denham could contain his curiosity no longer. The *Gustavus Adolphus*, the old Swedish contraband coaster that worked for British Intelligence, never used code – the old tub's rough-and-ready crew wouldn't be up to that. But whoever Sparks was receiving was using code. So who was it? That was the question he posed to the operator during a brief break while Sparks turned the page of his message pad.

Sparks, keen-eyed and flushed with excitement himself, looked across at Denham, still listening to the signal, saying, "No names have been given – only a code signal for the name of the ship in question, sir. But I can make an educated guess."

"Who?"

"I think I can recognise the operator's hand . . . I don't know what—"

"For Chrissake, man," Denham almost screamed at the operator. *"Who?"*

"I think – no, I'm certain, sir, it's the chief operator from the *Gotland*."

"You mean the Swedish cruiser?"

"I do, sir."

For what seemed an age Denham stared at the young rating, his flushed excited face in what seemed to be total disbelief. Then, as calmly as he could, he said, "Sparks, please give me the message. I'll start decoding it, the best I can, *now*."

Numbly the rating handed the message pad over, while Captain Denham started to fumble in his tunic for his glasses. He didn't yet know the meaning of the encoded message which they had inadvertently picked up from the neutral Swedish cruiser, but what he did know was that the message was so erratic and jumbled, the operator who had sent it must have been drunk, mad, or frightened out of his wits.

Eleven

The motor launch had glided the last couple of hundred metres towards the anchored Swedish freighter, her outline barely glimpsed through the rolling morning mist. Even her riding lights had been extinguished – something which contravened the maritime navigational code, Klaus von Kadowitz knew. It was obvious the unknown Swedish skipper had done so in order to conceal the position of his ship. The knowledge strengthened the young officer-cadet's belief that the Swedes were up to no good.

Metre by metre they had come closer to the rusty old coaster, with the crew of the motor boat, tense with expectancy, holding their weapons. Hansen was taking no chances with those 'treacherous Swedish slime-shitters' and had ordered the men to arm themselves – in hands that were damp with sweat despite the dawn cold. When they had been within fifty metres or so of the Swedish ship's stern, Klaus had begun to feel they were going to take her by surprise. He reasoned that the Swedish lookouts would be up on the forward deck, watching for the passing of the *Prinz Eugen* and her attendant destroyers.

But the young officer-cadet had been proved wrong.

Suddenly – startlingly – an angry voice had challenged them in Swedish from somewhere to the stern. For a moment on the tiny bridge he and Hansen had been paralysed, unable to act, wondering what the challenge in Swedish had meant.

Hansen recovered first. He cried in his rough North German accent, "German Navy. Identify yourself!"

Now it was the turn of the Swedes to be surprised. But when the original voice replied and they caught a glimpse of a broad, bearded face peering down at them through the rolling wet mist, the answer was definitely defiant.

"*Hau doch ab, Mensch!*" the Swede cried in good German. "These are international waters—"

"And this is a German machine gun." Hansen cut him short. "Try this on for frigging collar size." He pressed the trigger of the Schmeisser machine pistol clutched to his side.

The little machine gun leapt into angry life. Suddenly the damp air was full of the stink of burnt cordite. Tracer zipped lethally towards the Swedish ship. The Swede cursed and ducked. A pattern of holes was stitched along the plates where his big head had just been seen. Bits of gleaming shattered metal showered his ducked shoulders. "Now then," Hansen yelled, voice no longer so angry. "Are yer frigging well gonna talk turkey, you frigging arse with ears?"

Just for a moment Klaus thought the 'arse with ears' might. But he was mistaken.

Plop! With a sudden hush, a flare hissed into the grey sky. It traversed the length of the little motor boat in a green-glowing curve. *Whoosh*! It exploded.

Instantly they were bathed in a green-glowing, eerie, unnatural light. Hansen cursed and Klaus shielded his eyes against the abrupt blinding glare of that incandescent flame that hovered above them momentarily like some strange angel.

"What in three devils' name—" he began.

The Swede – later Klaus discovered that it was the contraband runner's skipper – cut him off. "Now you can see who you're talking to, eh?" Before Klaus had a chance to object, the angry Swede beat him to it with, "A neutral Swedish ship, going about her business in international waters—"

"Yeah, you neutral ape turd." Hansen's voice was filled with real anger. "Selling out honest German sailors' lives for them precious Swedish kroner of yourn."

The Swedish skipper ignored the interruption. "I've already signalled the Swedish cruiser *Gotland*. She'll be on her way here soon. Then you'll cop it, sailor boy." There was no denying the sneer in the Swede's voice as he recognised Klaus von Kadowitz as the skipper of the little German Navy boat. "If I was you, I'd pick up me hindlegs in me hands and make a run for it before our boys in blue come and blow you German pigs out of the water." He turned at the rush of heavy boots running from amidships. At least a dozen sailors were coming towards him, all armed with some sort of weapon. "Perhaps, though, we might do it ourselves," he added. "Bunch of shitting kids like you, still wet behind the spoons . . . Easy as falling off a frigging log."

Hansen, angry beyond all measure, pressed the trigger of the machine gun, which he held in those steam-shovel paws of his as if it were a child's toy. It burst into crazy life. This time he aimed to kill.

Behind the contemptuous bearded figure of the Swedish skipper, a crew member was hit. A series of blood-stained buttonholes had been suddenly stitched across his chest. He screamed, high and hysterical, and his shotgun clattered to the deck. Madly he clawed the air in his dying frenzy. It was as if he were attempting to climb the rungs of an invisible ladder, his eyes fixed pleadingly on the heavens. But on this cold foggy morning in the Baltic, God was looking the other way. Next instant the man fell face forward on to the blood-slickened deck. He was dead before he slammed into it.

Almost immediately all hell had broken loose. The Swedes had opened fire at once. A ragged, but potentially lethal volley swept the little boat bobbing up and down on the wavelets below.

A young signaller cursed angrily. Almost as if in surprise that it was happening to him, he stared in shocked silence for a moment at his shattered arm, the bone gleaming like polished white ivory through the gory scarlet mess of torn flesh. Then he fell.

That seemed to be the signal for the German crew to react. Klaus barked an urgent signal down to the engine-room artificer and the motor boat surged forward once more. As he tossed the little wheel from one side to the other with crazed energy, the slugs striking the sea water on both sides of her, the young sailors began to fire back, Hansen yelling wildly, "That's it, you bunch o' cardboard seamen! Kick 'em in the bollocks. Slap 'em in the chops. Show them Swedish slime-shitters what *real* Germans are like!"

And that was what the 'real' Germans did. Klaus ignored the slug which shattered the glass protective screen of the bridge, showering him with glass shards. His blood was up. He was carried away by the wild, mad, unreasoning primeval urge of mortal combat. Later he could have sworn that he had been laughing almost hysterically all the while like a man demented.

He slammed the boat against the hull of the coaster just near the forward ladder. *"Los, Männer,"* he cried, "board her!"

"Get your frigging pansy arses outta a sling," Hansen snarled and ripped off another wild burst. A Swedish seaman trying to emerge from the forward deck hatch went down screaming, arms flailing in the air in his absolute unbearable agony, what looked like a handful of strawberry jam spilling down his shattered face.

The men needed no urging. As Hansen covered them, standing legs astride on the swaying deck, firing controlled bursts to left and right like some cowboy gunslinger in a Hollywood western, they scrambled up the ladder. They jostled each other for a foothold and hit the deck up top. They fired, wildly cheering all the while like a bunch of excited kids suddenly released from school after a boring day.

The Swedes tried to press forward. Hansen didn't give them a chance. He kept firing, holding them at bay, while at the quick-firer the two ratings brought the gun round frantically, training her on the Swedish ship's superstructure and bridge.

Klaus realised it was time to act. Soon his youngsters would begin to take casualties. He couldn't wait for that. He grabbed the loudhailer and shook off the shattered glass shards urgently. He pressed the power button and the instrument came to life with a hollow boom.

"Now listen to this . . . now listen to this," he cried through the instrument, using the traditional German Navy formula, the boom drowning out the angry snap and crackle of the small-arms battle raging on the deck above him. "Cease firing immediately . . . Cease firing and nothing will happen to you . . . Cease—" His words ended in a yelp of pain as a slug struck the base of the loudhailer.

The power went immediately. The electric shock swept up his arm rapidly, painfully. "Dammit!" he yelled in exasperation and, drawing his own pistol, fired six shots rapidly and without aim at the coaster's bridge.

That did it. It seemed to be the last signal – an unspoken command – for Hansen. He rose to his feet. Ignoring the slugs stitching a crazy pattern of sudden death at his flying feet, he raced forward. "Follow me . . . follow me," he yelled, using the traditional formula. "Follow me – *the captain's got an hole in his arse!*"

They followed, whether the statement was true or not, and five minutes later it was all over, with the young men, chests heaving still as if they had just run a great race, their eyes sparkling and bulging wildly as if they were drugged, racing through the ship, plundering and destroying, cramming their mouths full of good Swedish chocolate, thrusting looted American cigarettes into the pockets of their reefer jackets – for a while absolutely out of control.

It was then that Hansen discovered the women: the one still crouched over the radio transmitter sending as if her life depended upon it; the other, blonde and beautiful, but obviously very drunk, hiding behind the bunk in the radio shack, drinking straight out of a litre bottle of potent *aquavit*.

The sight stopped him in his tracks. *"Phew,"* he breathed, pushing his helmet back from his red puckered brow, "as I frigging live and breathe!" Suddenly he registered the sight of the woman hunched above the transmitter. He slammed the butt of his Schmeisser down on the top of the radio. It shattered, its valves snapped and the transmitter died with a short electronic moan. The operator began to sob as if her very heart was broken.

It was thus that Klaus von Kadowitz discovered them a few moments later, grouped there as if frozen for eternity like third-rate players at the end of a fourth-rate melodrama. For a moment he was tempted to ask what was going on. Then he thought better of it. It was quite clear what had happened here.

For what seemed an eternity, all remained silent save for the sound of the operator crying, while the beautiful blonde stared up at him from her useless hiding place, bottle still raised to her full lips. Then Hansen said, "What are we going to do with them, sir?"

"How do you mean, Obermaat."

Hansen licked his lips thoughtfully. "God, it's a waste. But—"

"D'you mean . . ." Klaus blurted out, aghast. The full

realisation of what Hansen was saying hit him with an almost physical blow.

"Well, it's obvious, sir, isn't it?"

"Obvious – I do—" But before he could finish the objection which had sprung to his lips instantly, the one who had been crying looked up and said thickly in German, "What will you do with us?"

Hansen tapped the butt of his machine pistol significantly. The two woman started. They knew what the gesture meant well enough. Hansen spoke a moment later and made it even clearer. "Dead men tell no tales, sir," he said in a low voice.

"*No!*" The blonde spoke at last. "Please no, gentlemen."

Hansen ignored her, though it was hard to do so. *Holy mackerel*, a little voice at the back of his head whispered, *she's worth a sin – or two*. He silenced the voice. "We've got to do something, sir."

"No," Klaus said sternly. "It wouldn't be honourable, would it. They're women, after all."

"*Honourable?*" Hansen sneered. "What does that matter in war? You wait, sir – I've seen it all before in the old war. Before this little lot is over, they'll be killing men, women and kids by the thousand – the hundred thousand – and they won't give a wet fart about it."

"You're wrong – and even if you were right, which you aren't, it does not matter to me," Klaus von Kadowitz said sternly. "We do it my way, whatever the outcome."

"The big shots up top won't like it, sir."

Klaus ignored the interruption. "They go in the boats – the women first. Then we open the seacocks. That'll give our people the time they need, you know, and it will give them a chance to reach the coast safely."

"As you say, sir," Hansen said easily. He jerked his machine pistol at the two women. "All right, ladies. Follow me."

As if in a trance they followed him, but both glanced significantly at Klaus as they brushed by him and went up top.

The boy didn't seem to notice. He was too concerned with his own thoughts. Perhaps even then, still 'wet behind the spoons' as Hansen would have put it, he realised that this was the last time; from now onwards he would have no further chance to indulge himself in what could only be called a conscience. The good, innocent days were over for him.

Twelve

Admiral Tovey of the Home Fleet was worried. The tall, rangy admiral with the big nose looked around the circle of his staff officers, hurriedly flown into Scapa this very dawn, and announced in as calm a voice as he could muster, "Gentlemen, I think I can safely say that the balloon is about to go up in northern waters."

If he had expected an excited reaction to his announcement, Sir John Tovey would have been disappointed. His staff officers were all seasoned old salts – they had been used to 'the balloon going up' ever since September 1939 – which now seemed another age. Besides, they were tired. Most of them, save those permanently stationed in Scapa, had been rushing around on fact-finding missions to Portsmouth, Plymouth, Tilbury, Bristol, Harwich, Hull and all the other naval ports, trying to ascertain the readiness of Britain's hard-pressed navy. They were simply worn out.

Admiral Tovey acknowledged the fact with a slight smile and the words, "I know you're knackered, gentlemen; arranging those damned Atlantic convoys month in and month out has knocked the stuffing out of the best of us." He gave a little sigh, something unusual in such a stiff, old-fashioned officer. "But I'm afraid it's once more into the breach – what nonsense Shakespeare wrote. After all, the PM's breathing hard and fierce down my neck."

Some of them obliged their chief with a faint laugh, tired as they were.

It pleased him for a moment, and then his long face hardened and he got down to business. "Well, gentlemen, if our suspicions are correct, at least our troubles will be large ones, instead of worrying about freighters that should have long gone to the knacker's yard and their cargoes of Spam. With luck we're going to add to the glorious tradition of the Senior Service." He frowned. "But I must confess that luck is going to have to play a large role in the drama which I think will soon be performed on our very own doorstep." He paused for effect, then he let them have it as if he were ordering a tremendous broadside from one of the armoured giants that were stationed, antiquated as they were, at Scapa. "We think the *Bismarck* – and perhaps the *Prinz Eugen*, too – are coming out."

"Great balls of fire!" the skipper of the *Norfolk* exclaimed above the sudden excited buzz occasioned by Tovey's announcement. "This is going to be some party, sir!"

Tovey looked grim. "It's going to be no walk-over, Bob," he warned. "We know little about the *Bismarck* – we didn't expect her to complete her running-in so soon – but we do know this. She is, our experts believe, the most powerful ship in the world. All we've got to touch her is a superiority in numbers. So . . ." he let his words sink in for a moment and watched as the smile and enthusiasm vanished from the face of the *Norfolk*'s skipper as quickly as they had appeared, "that's why you are here. To inform me of how many ships we are able to put to sea ready for battle within the next forty-eight hours."

"We've got that amount of time, sir?" someone asked from the back of the group of senior officers. Tovey thought it was the captain of the brand new *Prince of Wales*.

"Yes, I think so. The first indication of her position has come via Godfrey of Naval Intelligence through his chap in Stockholm – Denham. Early this morning there seems to have been some sort of a shindig between a German craft and one of our spy ships run by Denham. We guess the business is connected with an attempt by the *Bismarck* to sail the Baltic."

"And her objective, Sir John?" someone else asked.

"Search me," he answered a little helplessly. "But we can make an educated guess." He turned to the big map which covered one wall of his office and reached for the pointer with a practised hand.

"Incident reported by Denham in Stockholm reckoned to be about *here* at zero seven hundred hours . . . just off Travemünde."

They nodded their heads. All of them had studied the Baltic, in which German fleets had lurked ever since the Prussian Navy had been founded back in the middle of the nineteenth century, right back from their days as midshipmen at Dartmouth. They knew the inland sea well.

"So I don't have to tell you how long it would take the *Bismarck*, travelling at convoy speed and in shallow coastal waters, to reach, say, Bergen *here*." Again he tapped the map with his pointer. "So what does that mean to us?"

He answered his own question. "We have some thirty-six hours or so before she sails on the tide from Bergen, heading" – he stopped short and shrugged – "God knows where. But we'll come to that problem when we have to deal with it. First things first."

"As soon as we locate the *Bismarck*, we try to delay her for as long as possible?" Commander Rotherham of Coastal Reconnaissance, the lowest-ranking officer among all the brass, dared to comment when no one else reacted.

Tovey wasn't offended. "Exactly, Rotherham. Good point. We will be unable to assemble *all* our forces to meet the *Bismarck* – and *sink* her," he added, irony suddenly in his voice, "within thirty-six hours. So we must delay her. Coastal Command is already out looking for her."

"And then, sir?" the skipper of the *Norfolk* ventured.

"Then we send in the Swordfish." He forced a smile. "The old stringbags."

Inwardly Rotherham groaned. The torpedo biplanes were hopelessly obsolete. Loaded with a two-ton torpedo, it took the biplane all its power to reach a speed of one hundred knots an hour. The 'stringbags', as the Fleet Air Army pilots called their old-fashioned planes affectionately, were easy targets for even the slowest of the enemy's fighters. The attack on the *Bismarck* – unless they caught the most powerful ship at sea by surprise – would be a suicide mission.

Tovey caught the younger officer's look of dismay at

his announcement about the 'stringbags', but he didn't comment. He couldn't. It wasn't navy policy. Besides, if he forced himself to consider the deficiencies of the Royal Navy due to the parsimony of pre-war governments, he'd probably shoot himself. There were deficiencies everywhere. Even the pride of the fleet, the *Hood*, was a problem—

He stopped himself short mentally. That was a secret, a great state secret. He would not even allow himself to *think* about HMS *Hood*. But aloud he said, "Now we come to the *Hood*."

The faces of the assembled officers brightened. They were all proud of the great battle cruiser which had been the world's largest warship until the German battleship, the bloody *Bismarck*, had come along. Still, all of them believed firmly that the *Hood* could still outfight the German ship that was nearly a quarter of a century younger than she was.

"Naturally the *Hood* is going to be our first line of attack," Tovey said with more confidence than he really felt. "She'll get on the scene of the action faster than any other of our ships and she'll be able to hold the *Bismarck* – and more – until the Home Fleet arrives."

"Here, here . . . well said, sir." There were murmurs of agreement on all sides and Tovey's lean face lit up momentarily as he told himself that when it came down to it, these senior officers, all normally as temperamental as a lot of opera divas, would rally around the flag loyally.

"But a word of warning. We can't let the *Hood* tackle the Hun for too long without support." Tovey's smile vanished. "I expect every man here, whether in a sea command or on the beach in a staff function, to do his utmost to hasten the gathering of the fleet. That is absolutely vital."

A few of the attendant officers looked mystified. Why should the fleet commander be so concerned that HMS *Hood* not be left alone too long in the coming fight with the *Bismarck*? Surely the great battle-cruiser could match the Hun shot for shot! But they didn't comment on the little mystery. Instead they snapped to attention, as if they would be expected to leave to carry out Tovey's orders immediately.

They were not mistaken. A minute or two later Tovey said, urgent and imperative, "You know what to do, gentlemen. Please go and do it – and don't leave the *Hood* out there too long, I beg you." With that he bent his head over the papers on his desk, as if the men were no longer there.

A few shuffled their feet. One or two put on their caps and saluted a little hesitantly, while the rest waited uncertainly. But when they realised the Admiral was going to say no more to them, they started to file out.

In the bay, the 'stringbags' were lining up on the flight deck of the force's sole aircraft carrier, engines already started, flares begining to shoot into the grey northern sky from the bridge, as they prepared for take-off and the suicidal strike to come.

Beyond, the Sunderland flying boats of Coastal Command were waddling out to sea, all four engines blasting away, a wide white wake of boiling water following them. It was the second reconnaissance flight – the first had already been airborne for thirty minutes.

On the fleet itself men were smartly moving through the controlled chaos of the littered deck. All the hundred and one precautions and preparations for the battle to come were being made, with Marine buglers sounding off, petty officers shrilling their whistles and red-faced deck officers and petty officers crying orders at the matelots, while everywhere gulls were diving and rising, screaming shrilly as if in protest against all the noise and activity.

Tovey watched, sucking his ugly false teeth as he did so. He had seen it all before, many times, even as long ago as the Battle of Jutland back in 1916. But never had he felt this strange sensation of foreboding, even fear, which now sent a cold finger of apprehension tracing its way down his spine. Something was going to go wrong, he knew it in his very bones. But what?

Thirteen

Klaus von Kadowitz was in a quandary. The Swedish crew had obeyed his instructions without difficulty, though with much cursing. They had gathered their wounded and gone over to the boats while the excited young German sailors had opened the coaster's seacocks and then come back up to the deck, once more looting and wrecking as they did so.

The women, however, were different. They had refused to take their chances with the male crew members. The pretty blonde had protested in her good German, "But Herr Officer, we'll drown. They won't" – she meant the male crew members – "do anything for us. They don't like us."

"It's only a matter of, say, ten to twelve sea miles to Travemünde," Klaus had urged them, "and the wind is favourable. You won't even need to row, ladies. It'll blow you in."

But the 'ladies' had not been convinced.

Klaus knew he had to make a decision about the women soon. He couldn't be caught here, with a neutral ship sinking only metres away and the crew in their little boats not yet disappeared into the drifting fog that lay low over the still surface of the water. It could cause an international incident. When they had their victory later, and had swept the Tommies from the northern seas, as the *Bismarck* and the *Prinz Eugen* surely would, it wouldn't matter. But what in three devils' name was he going to do *now*?

The young sailors, gulping down their stolen Swedish chocolate and brandishing the looted bottles of beer and *aquavit*, which he'd allow them to drink later, were already beginning to man the boats which would bring them back to their own ship. Meanwhile the two women continued to sob, their shoulders heaving like two pathetic, broken-hearted little girls. "Heaven, arse and cloudburst," Klaus told himself angrily, "what a shitting mess. Why should I be shitting well landed with it?"

There was no answer to that particular overwhelming question. Even if there had been, there was no time left to deal with it, for now the young lookout in his little steel cage on the foredeck was crying in alarm, "*Aircraft* . . . coming in fast," and even before they were identified and the twin Spandaus behind him had hissed in high-pitched hysterical fury, Klaus knew they were English. The great break-out into the Baltic had been spotted already.

The next five minutes were hell. The great four-engined flying boats came zooming in all out. They seemed fearless. With their prop-wash thrashing the sea in their wake into a frothy white fury, they attacked at mast height, only ascending in the same instant that they dropped their bombs, with Hansen, too drunk to realise the danger, crying, "Now they're shitting steel on us poor sailor boys . . . what a shitting life."

128

But the 'poor sailor boys' were fighting back desperately. Behind the bridge, now peppered and splintered to matchwood with the flying shrapnel, the two gunners fired for all they were worth. They were no longer afraid. The crazy fury of battle had seized them. As they spun their air-cooled Spandaus, the brassy, smoking cartridge cases splattering down in a metallic rain at their feet, they shrieked and shouted, cursing fluently, obscenely, their one aim in life to strike back and punish those who were punishing them so cruelly.

A great wedge of gleaming silver shrapnel came hissing the length of the craft. It sliced and hacked at all before it. The radio mast came tumbling down in a mess of angry blue sparks. A dinghy went over the side and the compressed gas pumped into it exploded in a ball of fire, searing the length of the starboard side. Paint blistered and popped and great scabs appeared suddenly like the symptoms of some loathsome skin disease.

The left Spandau ceased firing. Klaus flung a look upwards. A headless corpse was lolling there, held upright by the steel retainer ring. Thick scarlet blood welled up in obscene bubbles from the severed neck. In the scuppers a head, complete with helmet, rolled slowly to a stop like a football abandoned by some careless child.

Klaus felt the hot bile well up inside his throat. He couldn't help himself. He choked and spluttered. In the next instant he bent and a thick, sickening stew poured from his gaping mouth.

"That's right, Oberfahnrich," Hansen yelled with drunken exuberance. "Get them cookies up . . . the best for yer. Spew 'em up, sir."

When Klaus von Kadowitz raised himself again weakly, gasping for breath, his heart beating furiously, the first Sunderland was coughing and spluttering on a westbound course, dark and dangerous smoke pouring from her feathered starboard engine.

He shook his head and wished next moment he hadn't. A stabbing pain – like that made by a red-hot poker, it seemed – thrust into the back of his right eye. He gave a little yelp of pain. This time he shook his head more gently. The red mist cleared and now he could see normally. Cautiously he looked at the departing Tommy flying boat and then around him.

Hansen was leaning weakly against the bulkhead. He stared with a look of total disbelief at the shattered bottle of schnapps below him. It was as if he were unable to comprehend that such a tragedy should have happened to him. Klaus began to give a weak grin.

It died almost instantly as he gazed at the two Swedish women. They were still clinging to each other in total despair. But now their contorted features were set, frozen in a parody of great emotion for all time.

"Oh, God in heaven," Klaus gasped, carried away by the shock of that terrible vision. "They're . . . they're both dead!"

Hansen pulled himself from the bulkhead and dropped the remains of the shattered bottle to the deck with a clatter. His voice was no longer so hard and unyielding. Instead he kept his voice deliberately low. "You'll get used to it, Oberfahnrich . . . We all do – and if we don't," he added tonelessly, as if he were stating a simple truth, "we go mad . . ." Then his voice resumed its normal

harsh urgent manner. "The second bastard's coming in
– to starboard." Already the remaining machine gun had
taken up the challenge and a white-and-red tracer was
beginning to arc its way in a lethal morse towards the
approaching Sunderland. "I think we ought to get under
way. Like this we're frigging sitting ducks—"

"Engine room," Klaus von Kadowitz was already
shouting down the voice-pipe to the engineer rating
below, "both ahead. *Volle Fahrt voraus!*" He braced
himself for the shock.

It came in the very next moment, the twin engines
thundering into full power. The little craft shuddered
violently like a thoroughbred dog waiting to be let off
the leash. The nose tilted upwards. In the same instant
that the great Sunderland came roaring in, dragging
its evil black shadow behind it across the surface of
the sea, its machine guns chattering sudden death, the
motor boat shot forward. Behind its flying wave, the
first enemy bombs started to explode purposelessly. On
the deck, the two women, clasped in each other's arms
like star-crossed lovers, stiffened in the cold sea air. For
ever afterwards, the image of the two nameless foreign
women would symbolise for Klaus von Kadowitz the
absolute futility of war, which knew no victories, only
personal defeats . . .

They ran into Hamburg harbour that night, limping
past the familiar lightship *Elbe Eins*, struggling with ever-
decreasing power down the long haul of the River Elbe.
Finally they saw the badly blacked-out docks ahead and,
with their bomb-damaged engines gone altogether, came
gliding noiselessly to a stop at the great port's civilian

Landungsbrüke where a greatly surprised middle-aged policeman with a well-nourished paunch drew his service pistol and demanded to see their identity cards. This gave the survivors their first hollow weary laugh since they had left Danzig in what now seemed another age.

But their sense of humour vanished when Klaus and Hansen, weary, dirty and as bloody as they were, were summoned to the great port's famous Hotel Vierjahreszeiten to meet a certain Kapitän *zur See* Wichmann. He even sent a gleaming Horch staff car, complete with yeoman chauffeur and tin flag on the bonnet, to fetch them through the blacked-out streets to the hotel on the Innenalster, Hamburg's great inland lake.

The reception attendants stared at the two dirty, unshaven, bloody apparitions from the fighting front as if they were creatures from another world. It was the same with the elegantly uniformed senior officers – a few of whom carried swords, of all things, in the midst of total war – and their bejewelled ladies who sauntered in and out leaving behind them the sound of dance music, the popping of champagne corks and high-pitched tipsy girlish laughter. Obviously Hamburg's *Prominenz* were holding the usual May Ball – and were lacking none of the trimmings, including bowls of what Hansen whispered was 'frigging shoe-polish' and which Klaus knew was real caviare.

"One law for the shitting rich and another for the poor," Hansen commented out of the side of his mouth as he watched an elderly admiral feasting his eyes on the delightful low-cut cleavage of a girl half his age, his knuckles white as he gripped the hilt of his sword. "Get a load of him, for instance. He's going get a heart attack if he keeps on looking down her dress like that."

"Knock it off, Hansen," Klaus hissed urgently out of the side of his mouth. "This looks like the big cheese coming our way now." He gave a slight nod of his head at the officer now approaching them, one that, in his shabby naval uniform and tarnished gold rings, looked slightly out of place in that glittering assembly. But there was no denying the keenness of the officer's eyes, which almost seemed to spring from his pale intellectual's face, so unlike the ruddy, well-fed ones of the other naval officers and their young mistresses, who passed to and fro bearing their glasses of vintage French champagne that everyone who was anyone drank these days.

"Oberfahnrich von Kadowitz; Obermaat Hansen," Captain Wichmann snapped without any preamble, "report."

"Oberfahnrich . . . *zur Stelle!*" Hastily Klaus rapped out the standard, long-winded formula, standing stiffly to attention.

Wichmann nodded his approval. He relaxed a little. "Obermaat," he ordered Hansen, "go over to the buffet, help yourself to drinks and food for ten minutes, then come back with a drink for the officer. I wish to talk to him alone."

Hansen was so taken aback by the no-nonsense order that he didn't even attempt one of his usual bloody-minded objections. Besides, one of the girls behind the buffet counter, in her short black silk frock and tiny white frilly apron, was definitely giving him what he regarded as a 'come-hither' look – and she really did have 'bedroom eyes'. He hastened away to try his luck not only with the buffet, but with the delectable young blonde running it.

Wichmann waited till he was out of earshot, then took Klaus to one side and said without any further details, "As you have probably guessed, Oberfahnrich, I'm Abwehr, Branch Hamburg and Bremen."

"Yes, sir," Klaus answered, flustered. He hadn't guessed anything of the sort. Now he wondered why such an important person as this local chief of intelligence was talking to a lowly ensign. Wichmann soon enlightened him.

"Now what has this got to do with you?" Wichmann proceeded. "I shall tell you. When you reach Bergen tomorrow" – *tomorrow*? Klaus queried to himself. *With our shot-up motor boat we won't reach Norway by then, or the day after for that matter* – "you will have the ear of Admiral Lutjens for five minutes or so. He'll want to know the details of the air attack on your craft. It will be important to him. Now," he continued, without giving Klaus a chance to ask questions. He flashed a glance at the buffet. It looked as if Obermaat Hansen was wasting no time. He was bent close to the blonde barmaid, his gaze fixed firmly on the neckline of her low-cut dress, busily engaged in some ploy, presumably sexual, of his own. "From your point of view and perspective I am an important man. After all, I am a four-ringer." He meant his captain's four gold stripes. "In fact, I am only a very little fish in a big pond. And you'll have the ear of the admiral . . . I won't."

"I'm confused, sir," Klaus confessed a little helplessly.

"Bear with me and I'll enlighten you."

"Sir."

At the heavily laden table covered with delicacies brought from everywhere in the German-occupied New Europe, the like of which Klaus hadn't seen for years, Hansen was rubbing his horny palm down the maid's silken flank suggestively.

"I want the admiral warned. As you have already guessed, British Intelligence is on to us. That Swedish drifter and crew were in the Tommies' pay. Their report was followed up by the aerial attack on your own boat."

Klaus nodded his agreement. The pale-faced Abwehr officer was beginning to interest him.

"Somewhere, another aerial attack is imminent. We have that from our agents in—" He stopped just in time and again Klaus was impressed. Did Wichmann mean agents in England? He thought the pale-faced spymaster with the brilliant eyes did.

"Suffice it to say this, von Kadowitz. The English now know roughly what's afoot here in Germany – and they are taking corresponding measures."

"But what do you want me to say to Admiral Lutjens, if he sees me?" Klaus finally managed to pose his over-whelming question. "Is it about these serial attacks?"

"Yes. But more, Ensign," Wichmann snapped. "Tell him, in view of what Intelligence here knows about the English reactions, that we suggest he limits him-self to a fast hit-and-run attack on their battle-cruiser, the *Hood*."

Klaus was impressed. The Abwehr knew that the Tommies' greatest ship would take part in their defensive measures. He told himself that they must have spies in every naval port in the length of the little island. "And that's it, sir?"

"No, not quite." Wichmann flashed a look to left and right as if he was afraid he might be overheard. But the foyer was now empty and, in the sudden silence as the orchestra took a break, there was no sound.

Wichmann leaned closer and Klaus caught a whiff of the captain's discreet eau de cologne. "You fly to Bergen from Hamburg-Fuhlsbuttel tomorrow at dawn by naval courier. As soon as you are admitted to the admiral's presence and are allowed to talk, Ensign, tell him this." He leaned even closer and whispered his vital information concerning the *Hood* into Klaus's ear.

Harding and Horace

"**R**ussian generals take over," Horace the Obit cried in mock despair, slapping the *Daily Mail*'s headline for the benefit of the bored barman waiting to serve us at the Oporto. "Christ, I can see it all coming again. Gas masks, and Vera Lynn warbling – excuse me, *Dame* Vera Lynn *singing* – 'We'll Meet Again'. There'll even be dried eggs, courtesy of the People of the Free United States." He dropped the tabloid on the bar as if he were sick of the world, couldn't stand it anymore.

Behind the counter the barman said, "More grog, Cap'n?"

"Yes, more grog," Horace the Obit said, perking up immediately at the mention of his favourite subject – booze.

For a moment I watched him from the open door of the Shaftesbury Avenue pub which Horace still frequents through habit and in hope that he might meet a 'kindred soul' – of what type, literary or otherwise, I have never dared to ask.

He is very old now, though he didn't realise it or show it. He is still a star reporter interviewing 'Fabian of the Yard', Freddie Mills and the like. But he's very bald and his hearing isn't too good, especially when he doesn't particularly want to hear, which is most of the time. "The world stopped for me in 1969, a vintage year, laddie," he booms when in the mood. "By God, wasn't I spreading it around in those days! Now I live in the past."

I smiled at the memory of that – and of some of the things he had written since he had been demoted from the front page to the obits. Who else but Horace could have written of some poor old fart who had passed away, 'He was a well-known street-corner writer of short stories, who spent his last thirty years on a street corner in South Shields, carrying a knuckle-duster in his right-hand pocket to protect himself from would-be marauding Scots from just over the nearby border'? Who else could have written that as an opening paragraph, especially with that well-observed 'right-hand pocket'? He might have made it up, but who would have thought so after that particular detail?

But, however much of an old-style mountebank that Horace is, and however much he is given to large G and Ts, large scotches, large rums, indeed anything strong and large, he is a mine of information on people, his knowledge gained through the Fleet Street old-boy network, huge domestic history tomes, and his work 'tarting up' (as he phrases it) the contributions of the other anonymous obituarists with whom he works for the 'pound-notish' papers (yet another of his creations). For that reason I was visiting 'HQ', as he calls the Oporto pub, just in case he could tell me something about the *Hood* and its mysterious sudden demise.

I was not to be disappointed – well, not totally. After the usual palaver – "What's happened to old Leo? Things are not the same since he doesn't have his own outfit. The Oporto's gone to the dogs. They'll be having actors in here next. Lot of old queens," plus naturally another 'large 'un', the first of many – he got down to business.

He knew about the *Hood*, of course. Of *course*. (Horace tends to repeat himself for emphasis – an old cheap novelist's trick.) And he did. At one time or another, he had actually interviewed Viscount Hood, a descendant of Admiral Samuel Hood, whose exploits had inspired Nelson and given the name to that great, tragic ship.

"Hood had actually been at the launch of the *Hood* as a four-year-old," Horace explained. "Said his main memory of that day was being allowed three puddings to mark the occasion. Good memory, what, Duncan."

I didn't mention that it was Horace's memory that was good. How he manages it after having pickled that particular organ in various 'large ones' for nearly half a century I don't know. But he does; he has a better sense of recall than some top-notch Jap computer.

"Do you think the Viscount would know anything of use?" I asked, watching him pour another four pounds or so of my publisher's pitiful advance down that undoubtedly scarlet gullet of his.

"Dead," he retorted with a gasp and a satisfied yet direct smirk. I nodded to the man behind the bar. Whisky flowed, coins of the realm changed hands and we were ready for the next round of the Memory Game.

"One thing, however—"

"About Viscount Hood?"

"Yes . . . and don't be too eager, Duncan. It's unseemly in a writer," he chided me in that grand fashion of his which he adopts when the 'large ones' start to rise above what Horace the Obit calls 'that celebrated plimsoll line'. And here he always points to the left of his ample belly, where he wrongly supposes his poor old battered liver to be located.

"Yes, of course, Horace," I said, looking suitably chastened. "But—"

"He always followed the career of the *Hood*, you know. He even served on her as a midshipman. But when war came he went into destroyers and on to the staff of some admiral based in the Med. He happened to be married to the *Hood*'s captain's American half-sister, of course."

"Of course," I echoed, again admiring Horace's talent for slipping in these little nuggets, dredged up from some remote seam of his memory, which might have some value or might not. It depended, as always with Horace, on how you wished to interpret his statements.

"But I did gather, when I interviewed him in his old age, that the Viscount wasn't too happy about the fate of the *Hood*."

"Understandable, Horace. After all, he had a close association with a ship that was connected with his family and his distinguished ancestor." I looked at his bland fat face. No emotion showed on it. His lips had suddenly clamped firmly together like those of a truculent small boy resisting the efforts of his mother to force cod-liver oil or some other bitter but life-enhancing potion between them.

I nodded. The barman put down the *Daily Telegraph*, poured another large one without my asking for it and, pushing it towards me, returned to the *Court Circular*.

"Ta very much," Horace said cheekily.

I beamed, pleased. The lips were unsealed.

He looked at me, suddenly solemn and quite serious – for Horace. His eyes were now bloodshot, but not clouded. Indeed, one could have said they were remarkably sharp and keen for such an old toper – and as Horace often said of himself, 'a bullshitter of the premier class'.

"Your publisher has obviously commissioned you to do a mud-raker. With luck you might make *Panorama* – or even *Timewatch*. He has, hasn't he? Small advance – and big royalties, if you're lucky." He cocked his head to one side knowingly.

"Something like that, Horace," I agreed. I wasn't prepared to give too much away. When the need for large numbers of 'big 'uns' was upon him, Horace knew no shame. He'd flog his own granny to the devil.

"Intrinsically the story is priceless. Great defeat, followed by equally great victory of our chaps – brave fellows one and all." I thought that in his new enthusiasm, he might well burst into 'Hearts of oak are our men . . . steady boys, steady'. But he didn't. Instead he continued with, "Seeing off the Bismarck several hours later; an eye for an eye, what." He licked his lips pointedly.

I nodded to the man behind the bar, who sighed and, remaining seated, reached up. For one heart-stopping moment he looked as if he might be about to pass over a bottle and let Horace help himself. Thereafter my advance from the gent in the Gay Hussar would have decreased very rapidly indeed. Fortunately he merely filled up a brand new glass to save himself fetching the old one and shoved it along the bar.

He held up four fingers wordlessly. Another four readies had vanished. I sighed and hoped he'd finish what he had to tell me soon. Otherwise I'd be solving the mystery of the poor old *Hood* for nothing.

"I looked at it myself once, you know," Horace continued after wetting his whistle yet once more. "I got as far as you have probably got – I must say, I prefer the American 'gotten' here—"

"Oh, do move along, Horace," I protested.

"Well, as I said, I reached the point where the *Bismarck* knocked the *Hood* out so easily – even though the *Hood* was pretty well protected by additional armour which had been added to her over the years. So what had happened?" He answered his own question. "Was it the torpedo tubes at her sides, near to the waterline, both armed with torpedoes which were ready for firing when the *Bismarck*'s shells hit her? Did those torpedoes explode and send the ship and all the poor devils aboard her to kingdom come? Or was it the extra ammo that some people maintain was stacked on her deck at the time of sailing? Those, my dear Harding, might well be rational explanations. But," – he was almost purring now – "reality is a bit of a bore and can, at times, be downright dangerous, don't you think, Duncan?"

I didn't rise to the bait. I was running out of money – and patience – rapidly. One more 'big one' and that was his lot, *Hood* mystery be damned!

"So what do you think happened, Horace?" I put it to him directly. "Why did she sink so rapidly, after perhaps two salvoes from the *Bismarck*'s heavy guns?"

He looked at his almost empty whisky glass and then thought perhaps he had been bribed enough.

"Why did she sink so rapidly?" he echoed, chin raised like that of some great thinker waiting to be immortalised in marble by the sculptor. "Well, I shall tell you. I shall reveal it to you, dear Duncan, the great secret gained by sleuth from a paragon of the admiralty in the course of a long, hard drinking session at the United Services."

I could have shaken him. But I didn't. He'd last a few more minutes in his present state before he had to stagger off to the bogs. He'd have time enough to reveal all. So I waited on tenterhooks.

"It was the metal."

"*Metal?*"

"Yes." Suddenly Horace the Obit belched rather loudly and clutched his stomach as if in pain.

"Metal—" I began and then thought better of it. Horace was rising to his feet, bent slightly and still clutching his stomach. "Wind?" I enquired.

"More like a bloody tornado . . . on its way . . . old bean," he gasped, as if it took an effort of sheer willpower to get every phrase out. "I'm afraid I must leave you . . ." He farted now, long, loud and not totally unmusical.

The barman stepped back hastily and cried indignantly, "Hey, none of that, man! It ain't allowed in here."

"*Hospital?*" I cut his protest short, but I could see his point. His honest face was turning a very peculiar shade of green. Perhaps he was still not used to the noxious gases that elderly men release into the atmosphere while under the influence of the demon drink.

"No, you silly sod," Horace gasped. "To the loo . . . I must bid you adieu—"

He never completed the sentence. Instead, his lips clenched tightly together, his hand gripping his belly, he stumbled to the Operto's bathroom.

"Cirrhosis of the liver causing reflux," I said aloud to no one in particular.

The barman looked very worried. His hand reached out instinctively for his favourite tipple, rum. "Is it catching, Mr Harding?" he asked, hurriedly unscrewing the cap with trembling fingers.

"Not for a long while," I reassured him. "Give Horace – when he emerges – my best, please."

He shook his head and poured himself a stiff grog. "Not till all that green smoke he made clears. Now *that* is real dangerous." With that he tossed off the neat rum in one gulp. Then he shuddered.

Outside there was the usual long line of impatient taxi drivers waiting to turn left past the Oporto, hoping to catch the unwary and unsteady as they emerged from the doors of HQ. I saw Leo. He waved. I waved. "Ships that pass in the night," I mouthed at him, knowing the roar of the traffic would drown any attempt to exchange the usual civilities.

"Tin ear," he mouthed back and headed for 'headquarters'.

"Stimulating conversation," I replied, but already he had vanished inside to conduct those important affairs which engage the day of us city chaps, leaving me to dodge a taxi driver engaged in one of his usual midday kamikaze attacks and to wonder what Horace the Obit had meant by 'metal'.

Fourteen

Hamburg-Fuhlsbuttel Airport was empty, save for a few lumbering Auntie Jues, as the troops called the three-engined Junkers 52 transport planes. Hansen and Klaus both knew there was a red alert in place, but the fighters patrolling the Baltic and Denmark Straits on the lookout for English air attackers were already in position. And no one, it was reasoned by the Hamburg Flak District, would attack the city and its airport, not at this time of the morning anyway. As the flight controller had pointed out earlier when he had allotted them their seats in the Bergen-bound plane, "The Tommies will be drinking that awful tea of theirs still."

"Flyboy," Hansen had sneered when he had been out of earshot. "What does that rear-echelon stallion know about the Tommies?" He had spat contemptuously into the dust outside the flight control building, though without his usual energetic emphasis; apparently he was too weak. As he had remarked to Klaus during the long journey from the Hotel Vierjahreszeiten through the suburbs, along the Sachsenwald and towards the airport, "God in heaven, Oberfahnrich, first I had so much ink in me fountain pen that I didn't know who to write to first. Then she had me

146

going at it in bed like a frigging fiddler's elbow." He had sighed as if sorely troubled. "I swear she's shagged me impotent now."

Klaus had laughed. "I'm sure you'll get over it, Obermaat," he had commented.

"At my age, you've got to be careful . . . things happen," Hansen had hinted darkly. "You've got to be a bit careful about throwing it about too much; it could snap." And he had lapsed into a brooding silence as he considered that terrible fate.

But he'd cheered up at the airport, where the fat kitchen-bull had laid on such a spread for them that the other passengers, mostly officers, had stared across enviously. There'd been Bauernfrühstück, Stinkkäse – a whole heap of it – and real Bohnenkaffee, as much as they could drink, with a whispered offer of a schnapps for those who fancied the fiery liquor. Hansen, naturally, did and he had drunk half a bottle of best Steinhager in a matter of minutes, maintaining it was the only thing that might still be able to "put lead in me limp pencil, sir."

Whether it had or not, Hansen was a happy man by the time Klaus saw no less a person than Kapitän *zur See* Wichmann descend from his Horch and come striding purposefully across the tarmac towards the building, where Hansen was now busy finishing the last of the Steinhager.

"Look at that," Klaus exclaimed, surprised. "Wonder what the Captain wants at this time of the morning?"

Hansen followed the direction of Klaus's finger with glazed eyes. "Perhaps he wants to kiss us goodbye,

Oberfahnrich," he suggested. "The big shots are pretty good at getting rid of hairy-arsed old hares like us – me – so that they can die safe and sound in their little beds."

Klaus ignored the comment. Wichmann looked both purposeful and yet harassed, as if something other than duty was driving him. The young officer-cadet wondered why and concluded after a few moments that Wichmann had probably forgotten something important enough to come out here at this hour to tell them. It was only later that Klaus von Kadowitz realised that people like Wichmann forget nothing. Kapitän *zur See* Wichmann of the Abwehr had had this final fleeting meeting planned all along, but it had to be done in the fashion of Intelligence services all over the world. Nothing could be done directly; the oblique fashion, or so it seemed to Klaus, was the Abwehr's chosen means of passing on orders.

"Glad I caught you, von Kadowitz," Wichmann panted. "Thought I'd come to wish you well and remind you of the importance of your mission to Admiral Lutjens."

"Thank you, sir," Klaus answered, a little overwhelmed. Full captains in the Kriegsmarine didn't normally see off humble officer-cadets at this hour of the morning.

Next to him Hansen cleared his throat quietly. Klaus thought he knew why. The veteran skirt-chaser was warning him. There was something strange going on.

On the field, the pilots of the antiquated 'Auntie Jues' were warming up the three engines noisily. The air was suddenly full of the cloying stench of petrol. Wichmann raised his voice against the sudden roar. "They say there's a great deal of enemy air activity – they obviously know we're up to something – over the Denmark Strait and Southern Norway. As a result we have to be very careful."

"Do you think we might get a parachute, Captain?" Hansen asked.

Irony was wasted on Captain Wichmann this dawn. He shot the big, red-faced petty officer a stern look and said to Klaus, "If anything goes wrong . . . you know, I hate to paint the devil on the wall, but if you're shot down, I make you personally responsible for the security of what I've told you – and this." Like a conjuror producing a white rabbit out of a black top hat at an excited kids' Christmas party, Wichmann pulled a small, carefully wrapped and sealed package from his tunic pocket and pressed it into a surprised Klaus's hands. "I almost forgot this last night at the Vierjahreszeiten," he said, avoiding, for some reason known only to himself, looking at the younger man with those cool, calculating eyes of his.

Klaus felt the weight of the parcel. It seemed heavy for its size. But he didn't comment, save to say, "Will I have any trouble with security, sir?" He nodded in the direction of the helmeted Luftwaffe soldier guarding the plane.

"No; it's just a piece of metal, that's all, Oberfahnrich. Besides, the head of my service, Admiral Canaris, has taken it up with the Luftwaffe personally. Everything is in order." He clicked to attention and raised his gloved hand to the peak of his cap. *"Hals und Beinbruch,"* he said, keen gaze now taking in Klaus's face as if he might never see it again. "Do your duty. Report to the Admiral, as ordered. Guard that package with your life." His voice softened a little and the hand raised to the braided peak trembled slightly. "I envy you, young von Kadowitz." With that he turned and made his way back to the waiting car, his driver already gunning the engine, as if the two of them were in a hurry to get away from the little airfield for reasons known only to themselves.

"Funny one, that," Hansen said without much interest as they droned their way slowly up the Schleswig-Holstein peninsula, getting nearer to the old border between the Reich and the now-occupied Denmark. Within the hour they'd be approaching Bergen Field and the meeting with Admiral Lutjens, something that Klaus was not particularly looking forward to. After all, meetings between full admiral fleet commanders and humble officer-cadets still waiting to be commissioned were not very common.

"How do you mean?" Klaus asked, although he knew full well what the old boozer next to him in the hard leather and canvas seat meant.

"Coming to see us off like that. For a minute or two I thought I was for the jump-hooter right down hard in the brown matter – on account of that girl last night. I forgot to ask how old she was. Besides, one never asks a lady her age, does one, sir."

"One does not," Klaus mocked him, and added, "No, it was very strange indeed that he should come out like that."

Hansen tapped the end of his pock-marked, bulbous nose and closed one eye knowingly. "Wooden eye sleep not," he intoned, the customary phrase indicating that one should be always on guard.

Klaus nodded and closed his eyes as if to signal he wanted some peace. In reality he did. He hadn't slept much and now the monotonous drone of the engines was beginning to have a soporific effect. But he couldn't fall asleep. His mind was riven by the events and happenings of the last twenty-four hours and now this new problem which Wichmann had occasioned. There was something fishy going on; he knew that just as well as the permanently suspicious Obermaat Hansen, who was now beginning to snore loudly as if he hadn't a care in the world, did. But what was it . . . ?

A hundred miles further north, the little decoy convoy was beating its way forward at a snail's pace. The mixed group of German and Norwegian coastal freighters, all part of the great deception operation, were fighting a powerful icy head wind coming straight down from the Arctic Circle. Daylight had come later than was normal at this time of the year. A pale yellow sun peered over the heaving grey-green horizon, lying there as if exhausted and lacking the energy to rise any further. Every now and again the ships were buffeted by squalls of rain which turned into momentary snow flurries. It was a grey day in the grey part of a long war.

But the old salts, both Norwegian and German, who were manning the ancient, red-rusted ships, didn't mind particularly. It was now only hours before they ran into harbour. They hoped that, till then at least, the overcast weather and the squalls of sleet, snow and rain would keep the Tommy bombers off their backs, for the commodore in charge of the little convoy had already received a signal that English planes were cruising about looking for targets of opportunity. They preferred not to be those opportunities. As the middle-aged commodore remarked to his Number One, "Heinz, we're going to be the sacrificial lamb – without the mint sauce. Let the Tommies blow us out of the water and then they'll go home out of gas and honour satisfied. Old Lutjens in that fancy *Bismarck* of his will then live to fight another day."

His Number One, a sensitive soul, had made no comment. He now sat in the stinking lavatories, praying hard, while above him on the deck the red-faced, drippy-nosed deck hands discussed their chances in what was surely to come.

The commodore's gloomy prognosis was one shared by Admiral Lutjens, as that doomed officer sat in his state cabin on the *Bismarck*, reading the latest signals and reports from the radio room. To his mind they were encouraging. In the main it was clear that the Tommies were collecting their fleet. They had already sent out their reconnaissance planes – the attack in the Baltic proved that – and their antiquated torpedo planes were somewhere over the sea between Scotland and Norway, too.

He drew on the long thin cigar which he allowed himself in moments of tension to soothe his nerves and told himself that everything was going to plan. If the Tommy dive-bombers could be diverted to Convoy 21, currently sailing north at eight knots towards the Norwegian coast, he would be a happy man. They would waste their torpedoes on the totally unimportant coastal freighters, their cargoes useless ballast, and fly back to Scapa. It would be in the intervening period, before the Tommies could refuel and rearm the Swordfish and get them airborne once more, that he would sail with the *Bismarck*, the *Prinz Eugen* and their attendant escorts. It would be the ideal 'window' for him to leave Bergen and disappear into the wild wastes of the northern seas. Then his major problem would be to locate the *Hood*, sink the 'Pride of the British Navy', as the Tommy press called the great ship and show a clean pair of heels to their fleet in the dash back to the safety of the French port of Brest.

He leaned back in his padded leather chair and breathed out a stream of smoke, the very picture of a contented executive in complete charge of his affairs a man for whom nothing could go wrong.

Outside the men prepared for what was to come, while further off double sentries, helmeted and with rifles slung over their shoulders, patrolled Bergen docks keeping the Norwegians as far away as was possible from the ships. Those who actually worked on the docks were members of the Quisling party, headed by the pro-German Vidkun Quisling. They, like many of their fellows, were loyal to their new masters.

Admiral Lutjens grinned at the thought. But he did feel a sense of pride, too. Germany, the one-time pariah of Europe after her defeat in the Great War, was the master of the Continent once more, admired and supported by those many Europeans who believed in the 'New Order', introduced by the Führer, which was sweeping away that old decadent Europe with its rich Jews and their decadent, allegedly democratic politicoes. As if democracy had ever worked!

It was at that moment that Admiral Lutjens, soon to die 'honourably' in battle, had his dishonourable idea. It was probably the thought of Europe and the New Order, plus the consideration of the futility of democracy, that brought it to fruition. But it came to him, complete and without any loose ends. Even as he picked up the internal phone and asked for the signals officer, he knew it would work – and speed up the arrival of that window he needed.

When the Chief Signals Officer answered, Lutjens wasted no time. "Please dispatch this signal as an 'immediate'," he barked in that no-nonsense manner of his.

"Herr Admiral?"

"Signal Commodore commanding Convoy 21 *stop* please report your position at once *stop* plus estimated time of arrival Bergan *stop* Lutjens *stop*."

He could hear the signals officer gasp slightly at the other end of the line. "I'll have to use our top-level cipher on this one, sir. It'll take at least an hour to encode."

"*Immediate!*"

"But if we use our normal signals code, sir, the Tommies'll crack it before you can blink an eyelid. If you'll forgive the expression."

"*Immediate,*" Lutjens barked once more in a voice that brooked no opposition. He waited no longer. Slamming the phone down, he took another puff of his cigar. Soon the Tommies would know the position of the convoy and attack. They'd sink the lot, probably. But they wouldn't be too proud of the fact when they learned the nationality of the ships involved. It might well be another small-scale Mers-El-Kebir. At all events, it would be the window he and his fleet needed.

He grinned at his reflection in the mirror opposite. He was well pleased with himself.

At this point he had a little over fifty hours to live.

Fifteen

"Oslo," the second pilot said and pointed through the little square porthole to their right.

Hansen and Klaus bent forward and peered through the grey gloom. Beyond the stretch of dark green sullen sea there was the capital of the occupied country.

"The pilot's keeping well clear of the place," the second pilot, a handsome young officer with an enviable chestful of medals who looked even younger than Klaus, explained. "This morning everyone, including our own flak down there, has an itchy finger. He's not chancing getting a piece of home-made Krupp steel up his worthy senior lieutenant's arse."

Klaus laughed shortly, but Hansen, his head throbbing now from the night before, said sullenly, "What they frigging well filling their pants for? The Tommies'll still be waking up at this time, eating that egg-and-bacon muck of theirs. Fancy scoffing that kind of fodder at this time of the morning." He grunted and bent his head as if he were about to fall asleep again.

However, that wasn't to be. The second pilot straightened up as the Norwegian capital slipped away behind them and they headed out to sea once more. "The senior pilot's not risking flying over land. We're sticking to the briny. So he suggests you look beneath the seats and find those parachutes. I'll get the turret gunner to show you how to put 'em on in an emergency."

Hansen blanched. Klaus had never seen a man go so pale as the tough old salt. "Parachutes," he gasped. "Frig that for a frigging tale! I'm not gonna trust my luck to some old woman's knicker silk, Lieutenant."

The young officer shrugged carelessly. "Suit yourself, old house. If we have to bale out, you can stay behind and practise your driving." He laughed uproariously at his own humour and swayed and jolted his way back along the gangway to the cockpit, leaving Hansen to stare at his slim back aghast and open-mouthed as if he couldn't believe what he had just heard.

Klaus bent, grunted and tugged out the chute. He looked at it curiously. It was the first he had ever seen at close quarters. Indeed, this was the first flight he had taken.

For a while he stared at the gadget, wondering what it would be like to launch oneself into space attached to a square of 'knicker silk'. Hansen, for his part, didn't move. He seemed frozen to his seat, not even speaking. Klaus thought he had been struck dumb at the prospect of the parachute jump. That cheered him a little. *He* was not scared at the prospect, just bewildered.

But, scared or bewildered, the navy men did not have long to reflect on the problem, for they had hardly left the land again when the senior pilot's voice came over the address system in a harsh metallic monotone to state: "Starboard . . . it looks as if we might be in trouble. Get those chutes on, will you—" The rest of his announcement was drowned by the sudden hammering of the turret machine gun. Smoking brass cartridge cases started to cascade on to the deck in a bright golden stream.

The two men flashed a look to starboard. Set in two stark black Vs, about eighteen biplanes were progressing steadily towards the east, the heavy torpedoes slung beneath their undercarriages clearly visible even at that distance. But it wasn't the enemy torpedo bombers which were worrying the senior pilot. It was the two white-painted Sunderland flying boats that were flying almost parallel to the slow, lumbering Auntie Ju, coming in from both sides, their turret machine guns chattering frantically, sending white tracer hurrying towards the trapped German transport like glowing golf balls which increased in speed and intensity by the moment.

"Christ on a Christmas tree!" Hansen gasped, finding his speech at last. "The buckteethed Tommy barnshitters have got us with our dong in the wringer. How in three devils' name do I get into this shitting parachute?"

"Shut—" Klaus began. He never finished his command. His words were drowned out by the thwack of slugs repeatedly striking the fuselage to his right and above his head. There was the sudden acrid smell of burnt cordite and the plane was filled with bitter fumes that set Hansen off coughing. Next instant, the turret gunner came stumbling towards them, his hand clasped to the red gory mess of his face in horror, crying thickly, "I'm blind . . . comrades, I'm blind . . . oh, do please help me!" He stumbled and fell full length on the metal deck. He was already dead, the blood from his shattered face forming a pool.

Hansen pulled himself together. He turned the gunner over. "It's all right, mate, he gasped. "Don't worry. We'll see you're all—"

The words died on his lips with a stifled cry of horror. Where the man's eyes had been were now two suppurating empty pink holes. The burst from the attacker's machine gun had ripped his eyes out. Gently, for such a hard man, Obermaat Hansen let the dead man sink back on to his face, hiding that terrible wound.

Klaus was seized by a terrible burning rage. It was as if suddenly an emotional dam had burst within him and released a torrent of violent rage. He sprang to his feet, the danger, and the parachute that might save him if the worst came to the worst, forgotten. He stepped over the dead gunner.

"Where you going, sir?"

Klaus ignored Hansen. He swung himself upwards and into the gunner's turret seat in one and the same motion. He grabbed the butt of the Spandau and tapped the two drums of ammunition, one to each side of the deadly air-cooled machine gun. They were full and fixed tight. "Good," he said to no one in particular, while below Hansen still called, wondering what he was up to.

He peered along the length of the barrel and through the ring sight. The big white Sunderland was turning in a slow clumsy circle, its engines ejecting white smoke, clearly visible against the icy grey sky. He tucked the barrel more firmly into his right shoulder, one eye closed, jaw clenched pugnaciously. There was icy-cold murder in his young heart now. "Come on, you cruel swine," he hissed softly, staring at the great white four-engined seaplane, "come to Daddy."

The Tommy obliged. He had completed his slow turn now, engines feathered slightly before he gave them full power. All four roared mightily. The pilot, glimpsed as a white blur in the cockpit, poured on the power. He felt he had crippled the Junkers and its defensive ability now that the upper turret had been shattered and the gunner knocked out.

Klaus let him think so. He didn't dare miss. He'd let the great flying boat come as close as it could and then he'd let the engines have all that was stored in those twin magazines.

On and on the Sunderland came. It seemed to fill the whole horizon. The two planes were on a collision course. The German senior pilot was unable to take the defensive, since the Sunderland flying to port was just waiting for the lumbering, slow-moving Junkers transport to break in that direction and run straight into the enemy plane's full firepower. He'd blast the Junkers right out of the sky.

Klaus waited. He felt no fear, just a tense burning rage. Out of the corner of his eye he could see the enemy biplanes falling out of the sky, directing their torpedoes to a group of ships below. They wreathed the sky in deadly puffballs of flak. But the British sailed through that killing barrage unscathed. They were going in, come what may.

Klaus dismissed the planes and their target. The Sunderland was within firing range.

He tensed. "For what we are about to receive, let the

Good Lord make us truly thankful," he intoned in the same sombre way that Hansen and the other old hares would have done in a similar situation. He felt a cold trickle of sweat trace its way slowly down into the small of his back. It was almost the moment of truth.

The Sunderland shuddered. Smoke erupted from her turrets. Tracer arced gracefully towards the trapped Junkers, gathering speed with every instant. The fuselage trembled. Bits of metal and fabric flew everywhere. The Tommy gunners' aim was good. Still Klaus waited. He wouldn't get a second chance, he knew that. The other Sunderland would join in if this one failed to down the Junkers now.

Klaus von Kadowitz felt – as so many of his ancestors must have felt in all those battles they had fought for Germany – Fehrbellin, Jeng, Sedan, Langemarck and all the rest – that his personal fate no longer mattered. It was a question of doing something for the German race and the German Fatherland. If he had to die in the next few minutes then he would do so gladly, as had all the young men of his family who had done so before him. It would be an honour.

He took aim, controlling his breathing as he had been taught even as a youngster in short pants. "Lead 'em into it, little Klaus," his grandfather, the old Herr Baron, had always quavered in those long ago pheasant shoots, as he had squatted on his shooting stick, silver flask of some fiery liquor or other in his ancient, spotted hand. "Lead 'em in."

He did so. The plane grew ever larger. Surely he could not miss now? His knuckles whitened as he put the first pressure on the trigger. The world was exploding in front of him – a great white roaring mass, splattered with the crimson spurts of cherry-red flame of the hissing machine guns.

"*Jetzt . . . los . . . FEUER!*" the old Herr Baron's voice cried in his ears.

He pressed the trigger. The butt slammed back against his right shoulder, and he yelped with pain. The detonation slapped him wetly about the face. Madly the machine gun chattered. Empty cartridge cases cascaded to his feet. And then, before his eyes, as seen in some slow-motion movie, the attacking Sunderland started to disintegrate. Great chunks of metal flew left and right. Huge gaps were rent in the fabric. The cockpit shattered into a gleaming spider's web of cracked perspex. An engine stalled – and another. The plane's nose tilted. Frantically the pilot fought to keep control.

Klaus fired again. He felt no compassion – no mercy. This was war. The first magazine fell dead. Still the stricken plane came on. In a moment it would smash into the side of the Auntie Ju.

Madly Klaus fired off the other magazine. The Sunderland halted in mid-air. It was as if it had run into an invisible wall. Klaus tensed. A head-on smash seemed inevitable. But it was not to be. In the very same instant that the Spandau went dead and Klaus dropped the useless weapon, the Sunderland fell from the sky.

He gasped with shock, as if someone had just smashed a tremendous blow into the pit of his stomach. A white blur passed before his eyes as a parachute came hurling across his front. It failed to open. It carried an airman – minus his head – and was followed by another.

This time the escapee was alive, but he was screaming in silent agony, his face contorted beneath the leather flying helmet as the greedy blue flames licked higher and higher about his defenceless body. Then the great plane went into its final dive, with Klaus slumped on the littered deck, choking and sobbing, the nauseating bile running unheeded down his chin, his shoulders heaving in great gasps, while Hansen patted him like an overwrought, anxious mother, crying, "It's all right, Oberfahnrich . . . it's all right . . ."

Sixteen

Now alarm bells were ringing all over Europe. From Murmansk to Munich and from Cracow to Calais, everywhere there was hectic, even feverish activity. Telephones rang. Teleprinters clattered. Secret messages were encoded and decoded on the German Enigma. All seemed controlled chaos as officers and officials of half a dozen nations – those at war and those still neutral – discussed, decided and put into operation hurried plans for what was soon to come.

In fact hardly one of those concerned, outside of Germany's Admiralty on the *Tirpitzufer*, knew what was really afoot. But all *did* know that Hitler's *Kriegsmarine* was beginning its biggest and boldest operation since the outbreak of war nearly two years before. Even the Reich's 1940 sea invasion of Norway paled in comparison.

In the Kremlin the brutal dictator brooded while his officials brought ever more alarming messages about the Fritzes' activities close to the country's Arctic circle border with German-occupied Norway. The highest ranking commissars came and went on tiptoe, afraid to risk the wrath of 'Old Leather Face', as they called the pock-marked dictator Stalin behind his back.

For his part, Stalin sat slumped in his great thronelike chair, puffing at his pipe moodily, wondering if Churchill's latest warnings that Germany was about to invade Soviet Russia were merely provocations after all. This new massing of German troops in the Arctic could mean there was an attack coming from that direction on the key Russian port of Murmansk. What was he to do?

Others were in a similar quandary. Admiral Raeder of the German Navy was worried, too. He knew he was fighting the greatest navy in the world, the British, whose tradition went back five hundred years or more. The English Royal Navy had fought and, in the end, beaten every power in Continental Europe at some time or other. It had done the same with the old German Imperial Navy back in 1916. After the Battle of Jutland, as the English called it, the German High Sea Fleet had only once ventured to sea again: to surrender to the triumphant English.

Now, although the German ships were far superior to those antiquated British vessels, most of them dating back to the old war, the Tommies did have the expertise.

What if he lost the *Bismarck*? The Führer would never tolerate that. It would mean the end of the German High Sea Fleet, his pride and joy. The Führer would mothball his capital ships to avoid any further losses and hand over the war at sea to Admiral Doenitz and his damned U-boats. That ruthless bastard felt no allegiance to the navy as a whole. His main concern was the advancement of Karl Doenitz and his 'blue boys', as he called his sub-crews. *God*, he worried, head in hands, old-fashioned stiff collar already beginning to wilt in the steamy heat

165

of his office, *I could be on the damned retired list – or worse – within the week.*

The Führer was worried too. But not about the *Bismarck.* Up in his 'Eagle's Nest' in the Bavarian-Austrian Alps, the 'Watzmann', Germany's second highest peak, still capped with snow, which glistened and sparkled delightfully in the May sunshine, he was more concerned about the land campaign in Russia soon to come. Still, he did find some time for the reports of his naval adjutants. In between conference after conference he received them in the huge tea-room, sipping his peppermint tea, nibbling the sweet cakes he adored and farting all the while – for he no longer noticed the routine noxious explosions that came from his well-padded rear end any more; they had become too frequent and common. He listened to the adjutants' hasty latest summaries – "You have exactly sixty seconds, Herr Kapitän!" – and then dismissed them with an airy, "Just bring me victory at sea . . . that is all I am concerned about, my dear fellow." With his tail between his legs the messenger would disappear and Hitler would call to his mistress Eva Braun, concealed as usual behind one of the Gobelins, "What ponderous fellows these naval officers are. Still, they'll do the job. Now, what about a nice kiss for poor old Uncle Adolf." And she would fling herself into his outstretched arms with a squeal of joy at being allowed to be visible for a moment and hug him hugely.

For a moment or two the dictator, farting more excitedly now, and his mistress, in her Bavarian peasant dress, looked the picture of German middle-class joy. As the Führer often proclaimed in those halcyon days of victory, "What a blessing it is to be German and alive this glorious 1941!"

Churchill, a thousand miles away in London, was not so sanguine. He knew as much as he needed to know about the movements of the *Bismarck* and her escorts. It was not very cheering news: the world's newest and most powerful ships were being pitted against the world's oldest, though still powerful, ships of the King's Senior Service. Still, he was confident in the British Navy and her sailors. The days of 'rum, buggery and the lash', upon which he had always maintained the Royal Navy's reputation rested, were over. But the sailors were as good as they had always been back to the day of Horatio Nelson himself, though he had his doubts about the abilities of some of his admirals.

As he told his opposite number on Capitol Hill, President Roosevelt, a naval enthusiast like himself, over the transatlantic scrambler phone that May day, "The Hun has gotten" – he preferred the American usage; after all, he was half American himself – "too big for his boots, my dear Mr President. We shall beat them, despite the *Bismarck*; you have my word on it."

Roosevelt, no friend of the British Empire but still desirous of bringing neutral America into the war in order to defeat the German dictator, sounded a word of warning. "Let there be no defeat, Winston, come what may. It would only confirm those damned America Firsters of ours that the US would do better by keeping its nose out of a foreign war in Europe."

Churchill was ebullient as ever. "Never fear, Mr President, we shall win. You will take Uncle Sam to war yet. Lafayette we're here – *again*," he quipped, then, with one of his typical little poisoned barbs, "Then you will undoubtedly set about dismantling the British Empire." He chuckled at his own humour.

Roosevelt didn't laugh, but the men of HMS *Hood* did. They filed aboard the ship in their divisions, tugging at their caps under the wary eyes of their petty officers, laughing, making the usual old jokes about the 'lifers', as they called the former; young and happy, as if they were going on some pleasant outing, a gentle cruise perhaps, instead of possibly to their deaths. But then they were mostly 'HO' – 'hostilities only', young men who would serve for the duration of the war; men who didn't yet realise they would be facing not only the current enemy but that timeless one who confronted all sailors throughout the ages – the sea itself. Not until it was too late would they learn that the sea was the navy's most implacable foe: one that would show no mercy upon them once it had them in its grip.

"Look lively, lads," the petty officers urged, as they assembled in their divisions to listen to the skipper in due course. "Get them caps on at a regulation angle . . . move that fag from behind yer lug, Martin, or yer feet won't touch the ground . . . You there; you're on the rattle if you keep grinning at me like a pregnant penguin . . ."

It was customary banter that they had heard time and time again ever since they had joined the great sleek battle-cruiser, 'the pride o' the British Navy – and you remember it, mate, if yer don't want to lack a set of front teeth,' as they were wont to threaten in the dockside pubs they frequented on shore leave. But now the two thousand men who made up the crew were hearing it for the very last time. Those cocky boys, some as young as sixteen, were on their way to a rendezvous with death – and they went laughing.

Admiral Holland, the *Hood*'s skipper, wasted no words on the vast assembly as he addressed his crew for the last time. He wasn't a man given to unnecessary eloquence, even on occasions such as this. He stood there in front of his mike, hands stuffed into the pockets of his 'warm', a dyed-blue duffle coat, and barked, "You've heard the rumours by this time, I know. Well, they're true."

Next to him, his Number One frowned at the suddenly animated, excited faces of the young matelots as if warning them not to start chattering. The skipper wouldn't like it.

Holland didn't even seem to notice. He continued with: "We're after the *Bismarck*. The whole fleet is. We've been given the honour—" he paused in a dramatic manner quite unusual in such an austure man "—of leading that fleet."

Holland let the crew absorb the information, then snapped through the microphone, voice made even more harsh and metallic, "We shall be covered by an escort of six destroyers as far as the Denmark Straits. To the van there'll be the cruisers *Suffolk* and *Norfolk*. We'll be accompanied at some time in the next few hours by the *Prince of Wales*."

Someone gave a fat juicy wet raspberry but, although his Number One frowned severely, Holland let the sign of contempt pass. He knew of the rivalry between the crews of the *Hood* and the fleet's newest battleship.

Naturally he liked them to think the *Hood* the superior ship.

"As you can see, we will be well protected for most of this sortie. However" – his voice hardened once more – "when we find the *Bismarck*, we will take over and take the brunt of the action. It is our right – and, naturally, privilege – as the Senior Service's most important ship."

"Hear, hear," one of the teenage midshipmen cried enthusiastically, carried away by the excitement. Automatically the Master-at-Arms opened his book and took the blushing offender's name and rank. He'd be on the 'rattle' before this day was out. (In fact, he wouldn't. The fifteen-year-old youth would die with the rest.)

The admiral spoke a few more words, mostly dry-as-dust details of the sortie to come. Most of his speech didn't register. His excited young sailors were too concerned with the battle in the offing.

It was the same with the veteran 'three-stripeys' and petty officers, who had seen it all before. Some of the older ones had even fought at Jutland. They wanted to survive, and already their minds were working out the details of that problem. Some decided that they'd change into clean underwear. That way if they were hit, dirty cloth, which brought gangrene and other infections, wouldn't be forced into their wounds. Others concluded they wouldn't eat the traditional hearty meal before action stations. An empty gut was a good gut when you were wounded: again, it ensured that you cut out infection. Some told themselves they'd put a metal shaving mirror in their breast pocket. They'd all heard of the matelot who had been saved by the mirror when struck by shrapnel. (It had always happened to a bloke in another division.) A few prayed – but not many.

Admiral Holland muttered a few more words until his Number One nudged him and said, "Met coming through. Down in your cabin now, sir."

That did it. The weather forecast for the next few hours was vital. He had to hear it immediately; it might occasion him to change his plans. "Remember Nelson's words, men," he said with an air of finality. "England expects every man to do his duty."

It was trite, overused and something of a comic phrase to the more irreverent of the young 'HO' men. Still it stirred them with memories of another, more patriotic age, when men were not so cynical. Here and there they squared their shoulders, heads raised, chins stuck out defiantly like a recruiting poster of the ideal sailor, full of 'Jolly Jack Tar' and 'Hearts of Oak are our Men'.

Then the petty officers were trilling their pipes the marine buglers blowing their horns, the officers shouting orders against the wind and the sailors were marching away to their duty stations, with the admiral watching them for a moment. Observing him, his Number One was shocked to see tears in the Old Man's eyes. It took his very breath away. In all their long service together he had never seen the admiral give way to any emotion whatsoever. What was going on in the Old Man's mind at this particular moment? he asked himself, and decided that one day, when all this was over, he'd make it his duty to find out.

He never would. Like all the rest on the May morning,

with the fog rolling like a grey spectre across the flat sullen sea, he would soon rest in three hundred fathoms off the coast of Greenland.

Admiral Holland shook his head like a man trying to wake from a heavy sleep.

"Well?" he demanded of his Number One.

His second-in-command gave a little smile. "Fog, sir. Air reconnaissance couldn't get through as far as the Norwegian coast. But that's to the good, sir. Cloud as low as two hundred feet and the Norwegian coast blanketed in fog. Ideal cover for us, sir." He beamed at the admiral.

His smile went unanswered. It was as if Holland was preoccupied with other, more remote matters than the fog this day . . .

An hour later, the great ship sailed. In the old days, when she had sailed to show the flag at some other part of that great British Empire upon which schoolteachers maintained the sun never set, there had been cheering crowds, schoolkids waving cloth flags from Woolworths and marines, all sparkling brass and blancoed white accoutrements, coming to the 'present' with their bands blaring 'There's Something about a Sailor' and all the other popular ditties of the time.

Now the *Hood* sailed in secret, accompanied by the dour, eerie wail of a boy piper from the training battalion of the Black Watch, detailed to play alone and on the heights by his irate pipe-major. But even the boy, who would be killed at El Alamein, piping his battalion through Rommel's minefields to the assault, was moved by the sight of that great ship stealing silently away into the fog. Putting his heart into it and trying to avoid those elementary mistakes that had so angered old Sandy, the pipe-major, he piped that wistful tune that had sent so many of Scotland's sons away to die in some foreign field. "Will ye no come back again . . ."

Out in the loch, the great ship vanished into the fog.

Insomnia

W hy I always pick a hotel in Southampton Row when I stay the night in town is beyond me. I have known for years that the damned street is one long noise twenty-four hours a day. But I always stay there. Possibly the proximity of the place to Bloomsbury – and, naturally, HQ at the Oporto pub is the explanation for my unfortunate choice. Or perhaps some long ago nostalgia. I remember marching as a seventeen-year-old with hundreds of other reinforcements, five and six abreast, laden with rifles, helmets, field service marching orders, filling the whole of the fog-bound street that winter over half a century ago, just, I suppose, as my father and grandfather had done before me. I came back. My old grandpa, who I never knew, didn't.

All I know, whatever my stupid reason for staying there, is that it was a damn fool thing to do. Even with the skinful I'd imbibed with Horace the Obit, I couldn't get off to sleep. The noise was dreadful as usual – police sirens, screaming drunks and the homeless being evicted from doorways, and sundry foreign tourists. I was still awake and angry at my failure to sleep at two in the morning, with the reflection of some whirling police car light flashing on and off in neon blue warning on the wall of my bedroom.

At three, tossing and turning in the bed which had seemingly overnight developed a rocky surface at my most sensitive spots, I was still mulling over the mystery of the poor old *Hood*. My brain raced furiously, considering the various possibilities, while a hard little voice at the back of my mind was urging cynically, What the fuck do people care now? It was a different time. The people were different. Write anything you like – that'll satisfy the publisher. Think of that bloody piss poor advance. Knock it off, Dunc, and frigging well go to sleep, won't yer?

But it wasn't as easy as that. When I've got my teeth – what's left of them, that is – into something, I don't let go easily. Hack that I may be, I still have some professional pride, and there was a mystery here that I'd dearly love to solve. Naturally I could accept the traditional solution – that the *Bismarck*'s gunners had gotten lucky that May day so long ago, had hit the *Hood* in some particularly vulnerable spot and had done for her in that way. But if that was true, why wouldn't Kew release the documents for free use by writers and by the general public interested in such matters?

Or take the Ministry of Defence. Why were they so bloody cagey at this distance of time? What concern was that ancient battle-cruiser to them? The sinking of the *Hood* was merely a footnote in the long six-year history of World War Two. At the best, it presented part of the case for halting the construction of battleships, which were no proof against aerial bombs or huge shells which

175

could penetrate their poorly armoured upper decks. The loss of the *Prince of Wales*, sunk by Japanese bombers seven months later, should have been the final coffin nail. After all, she had been Britain's most modern battleship afloat at that time.

No, it had to be something else – something which still had relevance to the time in which we lived. Perhaps it was connected with politics? Political parties and prominent politicians still try to cover up their misdeeds and failings long after the event; and the successors in power continue to do so even when the people concerned are long dead.

For instance, I told myself, why are the papers concerned with the kidnapping of the two British Secret Service bosses by the SS in Holland back in November 1939 still kept under lock and key at Kew? What possible security breach could occur now, in the year 2000, if their contents were revealed? After all, the main participants have long since passed away – decades ago, in fact. But even now Kew sits on the papers of the Venlo Affair and will continue to do so till the year 2015, seventy-five years after the event.

But what politicians that sit in Westminster today would have any interest in the fate of the *Hood*? And what was that 'metal' old drunken Horace the Obit had mentioned before his hasty departure for the loo at the Oporto? If it had been of real interest – and could be connected to some current politico or his party – wouldn't Horace, with his eye for the main chance, have sold the story himself? Horace knows only one loyalty – that to the money which would buy him the strong waters that will keep him going till his raddled leathern liver solves his financial problems once and for all.

Outside two drunken Irishmen, perhaps ejected from the foyer at Euston in some pre-dawn police raid, were shouting at each other in the slurred toothless tones of professional meths drinkers. "Fight for frigging de Valera, that's what me old dad did," one of them was maintaining doggedly. "Old Dev, God bless him, knew a fighter when he saw one . . . ." They rolled away, taking with them that remote figure of de Valera, and a kind of pre-dawn silence settled over Southampton Row.

I sighed and then yawned. Suddenly I felt I could finally sleep and thought that I'd better bloody well get on with it now. An hour at the most and the place would be noisy as ever. I thumped the pillow, took a last swallow of my whisky and closed my eyes. I didn't pray. What's the use? I dreamt of York . . .

In the days of the *Hood*, York was not the tourist town it is today. It was a forgotten, dirty old place where the last event of any importance to happen to the ancient city had been its siege and capture by the Roundheads back in 1664. Now, the streets where we played as kids have long vanished. The local university has eaten up the farms and smallholdings and the like which edged right up to the city walls in that May of 1941. It has all changed, in short – but not for the better, places never do.

These days when I walk about the place, the street names are naturally still familiar, but the streets themselves aren't. They are peopled with ghosts for me – the 'Mad Major', a supposed First World War shell-shock victim, who saluted lampposts and pillar boxes, but who

177

was sane enough to be the local illegal bookie's lookout; the old gaffer with a beard down to his knees who rode a penny farthing twice as big as himself with surprising agility for such an old man; the 'basket case', the ex-officer with no arms and no legs, pushed around by his former batman in what looked like a long, shallow basket on wheels . . . They're all still there and will continue to remain there till I snuff it myself. Then they'll be finally dead.

And every time I go up March Street and stare up at the noble outline of the Minster to my front, the only thing of beauty in that tourist city, then and now, I remember her particular ghost. It has been with me nearly sixty years now, fifty of those spent in climes far away from that shabby provincial Yorkshire city – so I should remember that one, shouldn't I?

I can even remember the weather that May day when it happened. So you can guess the impression that her appearance, as she burst shrieking into March Street, must have made upon me. We were squatting in the dust, as kids always do, at some sort of loose end – what, I've forgotten now. Next to us the old printing works, with their German machines dating back to the previous century, were clattering away, providing the only sound save that of Old Abie, the rag-and-bone man, crying, "Any old rags, any old bones." If you were mug enough you'd give him the bits and pieces which brought good prices in rationed wartime England and get a gold fish back in return.

Then it happened.

A boy in blue uniform with cycle clips and a leather

pouch in which he carried the feared telegrams had hardly rested his red Post Office bicycle against the wall of the passage that led from March Street to the woman's house when she came running out, waving the message from the Admiralty.

She was screaming already, her iron-grey hair escaping from the steel curlers she wore, and her face was contorted by a kind of hysteria that I'd never seen before and which was frightening to behold. Indeed, Derek R, who would be killed in action in Normandy two years later with the Fusiliers, snorted, "Heck, the old cowbag's gone barmy." He must have been terribly frightened, too, to have uttered such a terrible word as 'cowbag'. In those days, boys swore very modestly.

There she stood in that dirty apron and oversized, laceless men's boots, waving the telegram like a flag, crying for her lost son. He had not been one of the three survivors of the nearly two thousand of his shipmates who had gone down with the *Hood*.

I can't remember her exact words now; too much water has passed under the bridge since then. But I have a strong impression that she railed against her fate that muggy overcast May afternoon while we stared at her in open-mouthed, shocked wonder. In those days, only mad women were allowed to have hysterics in public, especially if they were working-class. Hysterics and 'carrying on', as it was called, were only allowed for middle-class and rich females.

Afterwards, when the other women had ushered her inside with bribes of tea and the like, I thought about the matter in a boy's sort of way, trying to make sense

179

of her hysteria about something which had happened so far away. In those days there were tragedies happening every day. Men, women and children were dying by their scores, hundreds, thousands, tens of thousands all the time.

I couldn't even remember what her son looked like, save that I vaguely recollected a cap tilted at the back of his mass of cropped curly hair and a broad grin . . . oh yes, plus a gas mask in a canvas haversack slung across a navy blue chest. But in those days all sailors looked like that: cocky, grinning, caps at the back of their heads in a definitely non-regulation manner.

It was that 'kiss me quick' look; the way the sailors attracted the 'judies': Jolly Jack Tar, living for the day and bugger tomorrow. They were men without a care, blind to the cruel Nature that would face them soon enough, so it was, 'You'll get no promotion this side of the ocean, so cheer up my lads, fuck 'em all!' That was their style, doomed men destined for a watery grave.

In the end, all I could remember in the evening of that day when we read in a skimpy *Yorkshire Evening Press* the first details of the great battle being waged out at sea was that distraught mother's scream: that primeval cry of protest against a cruel fate which had deprived a widow woman of her single consolation for a hard, unrewarding life. Her son was now resting at the bottom of three hundred fathoms of icy water with nearly two thousand of his comrades.

I woke with a start. For one wild moment I thought I heard the stamp of hobnailed boots, hundreds of them, echoing and re-echoing in the stone chasm of

Sink the Hood

Southampton Row, heading for their appointment with destiny. But I was mistaken. The rattle of empty milk crates and the sudden drone of an electric motor told me otherwise. It was the local co-op dairyman delivering the hotel's morning milk for those who would soon be about, wanting their full English breakfasts and pots of tea, ready to go out money-grubbing for yet another day.

I tried to relax, feeling my heart beating fast, a little frighteningly. I could have done with a stiff drink. But it was only six in the morning and the mini-bar was empty. In an hour I'd sneak downstairs for an early breakfast – the very thought made me want to puke – and see if I could find a mini-bar with a miniature bottle – or anything alcoholic for that matter – still left in it.

I calmed myself and watched the sky over London flush from a dirty white to a soft pink, indicating that the sun had risen somewhere or other to the east. The Chinese say the sun brings enlightenment – or is it the Japanese? I don't know, but it does not bring yours truly very much in the way of a solution to the problem that had been bugging me ever since I had been conned into taking on the bloody book in the Gay Hussar. What a bloody silly name for a restaurant these days!

Still, it had to be solved. I owed it to the old woman with the men's boots. It was as simple as that.

I looked at my watch in the dirty white light. Six twenty. Good. I'd have a shower, shave and the usual. I'd be finished by ten to seven. By then the maids would be yawning, and beginning to think of rattling the cutlery to

181

waken their guests. By then I'd be downstairs and, having found the mini-bottle, be in the nearest lav savouring it and watching my hands begin to stop shaking. I started to feel happier.

Seventeen

Admiral Lutjens drew closer and closer to the enemy. Now and again through the rolling, billowing low fog he could catch a glimpse of the English squadron through his glasses. He knew Raeder, acting as the Führer's mouthpiece, had ordered he should avoid battle if possible. But with the English so close – and, by what his lookouts could make out, made up of an inferior force – it would be an insult to the Kriegsmarine if he made a run for it now. How would he go down in the history of the German Navy, which had so few traditions as it was?

Lutjens made his decision, while all around his officers waited, pretending to focus on the barely-to-be-seen enemy ships and identify them for the admiral. "Give permission to fire," he said simply, his harsh narrow face underneath the cropped black hair revealing nothing.

"Permission to fire," the senior staff officer cried. "I repeat—"

"Sir," the most junior officer, the one with the keenest eyesight compared to the middle-aged officers, whose vanity wouldn't allow them to wear glasses, cut in excitedly, "It's the *Hood*!"

"What?" Lutjens demanded. "Are you sure?"

"Yes, sir," the young Leutnant *zur See* said. "There's no mistaking her. She fits the recognition table exactly, Herr Admiral."

Lutjens' doubts fled. With what he knew now, he felt he could achieve a great victory with perhaps no cost at all to his own two capital ships. He did some quick thinking. "Run the permission to fire signal flags," he snapped, as his excited staff officers focused their glasses rapidly on the dim grey shape on the heaving, green-and-white flecked horizon while others worked out ranges and completed complicated calculations in their heads. All were animated by a frenetic mental energy. None of them had ever engaged in a battle contest such as this. If they won, it would be a tremendous victory for the German Navy, the Third Reich and Europe's New Order. Even Lutjens, not a demonstrative man under normal circumstances, told himself, brain racing furiously, Destroy the *Hood* and it will be an unparalleled signal that Britain's Rule of the Seven Seas is nearing its end. Once that takes place, it may well mean the demise of the British Empire itself.

He flashed a glance at the green-glowing, complicated dial of his gold chronometer, presented to him by the Führer himself. He noted the time very carefully. It was, in Central European Time, zero five hundred hours and fifty-two minutes. "Eight minutes to six on a May morning," he muttered to himself, awed a little by his own thoughts, "the end of the British Empire . . ."

"They're running up the 'open fire' flags on the *Bismarck*'s yard-arm," Hansen yelled in Klaus's ear above the thunder of the waves and the pounding of the *Prinz Eugen*'s engines going full out. He pointed to the battleflags beginning to run up their own ship's yard-arm in response.

Klaus felt a sudden emptiness in his stomach. It wasn't fear. Later he explained it to himself as the result of an overwhelming realisation that at this moment his young life was being changed by external factors over which he had absolutely no control. The change would be irrevocable. He would never be the same again.

"What are we going to do?" he asked himself – and Hansen.

They had reported to the admiral on the *Bismarck* and had then been shipped across to the *Eugen*. But their skipper had insisted they shouldn't return to their normal duty stations. He had declared them 'super-cargo', men with no job to carry out. Why, they didn't know. All that Hansen could say was, "It's something to do with that little box of metal you gave him, Ensign. I'd swear on it." And with that a puzzled Klaus had to be content.

Now Hansen, answered his somewhat plaintive question with, "Keep our frigging turnips" – he meant heads – "down, I'd suggest, Ensign. I think we've been frigging heroes enough for the time being, don't you?"

Wordlessly Klaus nodded. He supposed they had. In all his young life he had never undergone so many traumatic experiences in such a short time as he had done in these last few days. The dead Swedish women, the slaughter in the Baltic and all the rest of it, a lifetime of experience packed into a few hours.

Hansen opened his mouth to say something, but didn't.

Instead he stood there on the sea-lashed swaying steel deck of the *Prinz Eugen* with his mouth open a little stupidly. On the horizon bright red lights had blinked abruptly on, off, and then on again. For what seemed an age he appeared not to comprehend what they signified until finally he burst out almost as if with indignation, "Heaven, arse and cloudburst – the buck-teethed Tommies – they're – *firing* at us, Ensign!"

Holland focused his glasses. Down below the smoke from B Turret was drifting away, carried by the stern wind. The *Hood*, not the most stable of gun platforms at the best of times, was going all out. Holland was not taking chances. He wasn't slowing down to enable the gunnery officers to carry out a better 'shoot'.

Next to him his officers tensed. This was it. The first with the most would win this battle: all of them knew that.

Holland counted off the final three seconds before the great fifteen-inch shells from the *Hood* detonated, praying they'd find their target, in this case the *Bismarck*'s running mate, the *Prinz Eugen*. His strategy was simple. Damage the *Eugen* and she'd turn and attempt to get back to Bergen. En route the 'stringbags' would be able to deal with her at their leisure, whatever the cost in pilots and planes. That would leave the *Bismarck*, deprived of her support and the massive firepower of the *Eugen*. With luck the *Hood* would be able to see off the Hun battleship. If she couldn't, there'd be others to assist once the *Bismarck* started to make a run for it – which inevitably she would, he knew that implicitly.

"They're on target!" someone yelled.

"There they blow!" another cried on the bridge.

Glued to his glasses, Admiral Holland watched as the first shell exploded to starboard of the *Bismarck*, the target. The knuckles of the hand holding his binoculars whitened, the only sign of his frustration.

The second shell raised a huge spout of water between the *Bismarck* and the *Prinz Eugen*. Then it happened. The third shell struck home. A burst of blood-red flame, obscured a moment later by a huge cloud of whirling grey-brown smoke, and the *Prinz Eugen*'s radio masts came tumbling down in a frenzy of blue angry sparks. "We've hit her," Holland heard himself shouting. "We've hit the *Eugen*!"

"Bloody hell," an officer said in awe. "The *Eugen*'s bloody well slowing down, chaps. Oh my holy Christ, this is going to be some party after all . . ."

The scream rang out. It pierced even the roar of the explosion and the sudden hush of flame. Klaus shivered, as if with a sudden fever. "What in three devils' name—"

The cry died on his lips. A figure, one hand held in front of it like that of a blind man searching his way, appeared out of the smoky gloom, his body riddled with shrapnel wounds, the bloody gore flecked with smashed white bone that had been a human face dripping down the shattered skull like molten red sealing wax.

Klaus reeled back, hand held in front of his mouth. Hot sickening bile swept up in a flood from his throat. He retched. Next moment he spewed down the front of his uniform while before him that terrible apparition, glimpsed as through a shimmering red haze, trembled, reacted, failed and fell flat on that ruined face. A squelch, a nauseating squelch, and what remained of the dead man's features burst open like piece of overripe fruit.

Hastily Hansen grasped the reeling ensign. "Hold on, for God's sake, hold on!" he roared over the hollow boom of the guns. "Tuck in yer eggs and squeeze the cheeks of yer arse together, Oberfahnrich, it'll keep them in place." He flung a glance at the sailor lying in the pool of steaming red gore. "He's dead. *His* problems are over, poor shiteheap."

Hansen's rough-and-ready attempts to soothe Klaus worked. Weakly he shoved away the Obermaat's hands. "Thanks," he said thickly, his mouth sour with green bile. "Thanks for looking after me. I'll be all right now."

Hansen let go. "Nothing's too good for the boys in the service," he replied, using the current motto, his brick-red, tough face cynical once more. "I've got a flatman, Oberfahnrich, if yer fancy a snort behind yer collar stud. It'll put hairs on yer manly chest."

Klaus declined in the same instant that there was another whoosh like the sound a midnight express going all out makes when it roars through a deserted station. The two men ducked instinctively.

The great shell from the *Hood* exploded just to port. A huge wave of icy cold water swept across the upper deck, flooding it knee deep for a moment. Great gleaming shards of red-hot metal scythed through the rigging, bowling men over everywhere. A head complete with flak helmet rolled like an abandoned kids' football into the scuppers. Another rating was propelled screaming over the side, as if he had just taken a tremendous punch in the chest.

In an instant all was chaos again. Men were screaming on all sides. Someone yelled, "Mates . . . help me . . . I can't see . . . honest, I can't see." Fire control parties ran back and forth, reeling out their lines, while angry, red-faced control officers rapped out their orders, slipping and sliding on the blood-slickened deck.

Klaus pulled himself together. "Hansen, we've got to do something, do you hear. We can't just stand around like this."

Hansen forced a grin. "Don't worry, sir. Our time of standing around like spare dildoes in a convent'll soon be over. Don't you fret – the frigging war'll soon be coming our—"

His words were drowned out by the fire of the *Prinz Eugen*'s main battery. A great hot wave of compressed air swept the length of the debris-and-dead-littered main deck.

Automatically Hansen opened his mouth. The Old Hare knew that if he didn't, his eardrums might well be burst. Next to him, Klaus, in the shelter of a door, clung desperately to a stanchion as that tremendous blast of hot air plucked and ripped at his hold, trying to sweep him with it. It hit him about the face like a blow from a flabby wet fist. He gasped for breath, choking crazily like an ancient asthmatic in the throes of a final attack. On the deck in front of him the dead rating with the horribly shattered face was picked up by that great whirling tornado and swept away over the side as if he had never even existed.

Behind, the vanished detonation of those three massive cannons firing simultaneously left Klaus and Hansen panting and gasping weakly, hardly daring to believe their luck. They had survived! They were still alive!

They were the only ones. Those unfortunates who had been unable to find a solid hold had disappeared. The main deck had been swept as clean as it would have been before a ceremonial visit by the Führer himself. Nothing remained of the dead and the debris. All had gone.

Hansen broke the momentary heavy brooding silence. "God Almighty," he quavered in a shaky voice, for even the tough old mate was awed, "you can't hardly believe it, Ensign. All . . . all . . ." Suddenly he raised a knobbly fist that looked like a small steam shovel and waved it threateningly at the shell-pocked bridge. "You swine – you rotten swine . . . you got us into this. Like you did in the frigging old war. But you'll pay for it. I swear, if it's the last thing you do on this frigging earth, you'll pay for it." His whole body was shaking with rage now, his eyes bulging wildly out of his head like those of a man demented. Again he waved his fist at the unseen officers and skipper high above him on the bridge. "You'll pay, you bastards."

"*Hansen.*" Klaus grabbed roughly at him and forced that upraised arm down with more strength than he thought he was capable of. "They'll put you before a firing squad."

"I don't frigging care!" Hansen cried, his face contorted bitterly. "Why do they make poor old sailormen go through this misery? First in 1916 and again right now. Let the bastards shoot me. Ain't that what they're doing now, Ensign?" He stared at Klaus with those wild eyes of his as if demanding some kind of justice, understanding.

But Klaus von Kadowitz had no time for such luxuries on this cruel May day. All he knew was that he had to save Hansen from himself. He brought back his other fist and then punched it forward. It caught the petty officer squarely on the jaw. His head clicked and his eyeballs rolled back to show the whites. Next moment his legs started to give way beneath him like those of a newly born foal. Klaus caught him before he hit the steel deck. Gently he lowered the tough old petty officer the rest of the way.

Above them the turrets prepared to fire again, the battle pennants fluttering merrily up the yard-arm. Admiral Lutjens and his little fleet were going in for the kill.

Eighteen

Admiral Holland watched as the shells landed all around the *Prinz Eugen*. He knew that every second was precious. Yet for a moment or two he seemed paralysed, as if he were watching the battle in some cinema, settled down in a plush warm seat, really unconcerned about its outcome; as if it were happening to someone else.

Suddenly, for some reason he couldn't explain, he remembered that other May in 1916 when the buzz had run round the Home Fleet that 'the Huns are coming out'. He'd had a grandstand view of the Battle of Jutland, thrilled by that awesome spectacle. Later he had read that Churchill had felt that 'we could have lost the war in an afternoon'. Out at sea watching the battle, a sixteen-year-old midshipman at the time, he had told himself that they *were* losing it.

The German gunners had been better, their marksmanship and cannon had been superior and there had been something wrong with the British ships. What had Admiral Beatty snapped to his flag captain that day, with the *Invincible* sinking before his gaze? 'Chatfield, there seems to be something bloody wrong with our bloody ships today.'

Sink the Hood

Now, still in this self-induced trance, unable to act or react to the Germans only a handful of miles away, he knew there was still something wrong with the British battlewagons – in particular his own. It wasn't that they were all veterans, save the *Prince of Wales*, dating back to the Old War. It was their construction and the successive refits since the victorious end of that war, which had been aimed at making them match the most modern of German and Japanese fleets. The refits hadn't worked. The government hadn't been prepared to spend the money needed on Britain's traditional and most powerful weapon, the mainstay of the Empire, the Royal Navy. Now the supreme test had come. Could Britain still 'lose the war in an afternoon', as Churchill had recorded? Should he take the *Hood*, with her fatal flaw, out of the battle now while there was still time? They'd probably dismiss him from his command, perhaps even court-martial him, if he did. But what did he matter in the light of this momentuous issue? Holland wrung his hands in that classic gesture of despair and overwhelming doubt. God in heaven, what should he do?

But already that decision was being made for him. Five miles away, sixty-four German seamen – brawny and muscular for the most part, as gunners usually are – laboured in each turret of the four mounted on the *Bismarck*. Two hundred and fifty-six men, pale, sweaty-faced, their eyes flickering and their lips dried and cracked as if they hadn't drunk for a long time, prepared to open fire on the *Hood*.

On the bridge Admiral Lutjens waited for his chief

gunnery officer to report. He had already discussed the barrage on the *Hood* with the latter. The gunners knew exactly where to aim. Four times since she had been launched, the *Hood* had been refitted. Each time the Tommies had reinforced her superstructure with yet more armour. They had already begun to realise how ineffective their old capital ships were against aircraft and modern guns. But each time they had made the same fatal mistake, about which – thanks to Canaris – he now knew. Soon it would be up to the chief gunnery officer to make use of that secret information.

Admiral Lutjens forced a wintry smile. Around him his staff officers nudged each other knowingly. It was rare to see that hard, inflexible man smile. The Old Man was up to something, that was for sure.

In the four turrets the gunners waited, their guns loaded now. The call to action would come at any moment.

"Sir . . . *sir!*" The chief gunnery officer's urgent cry woke Admiral Holland out of his self-induced reverie. He shook his head, hard, whistled down the tube and answered, voice perfectly normal once more, totally in control again, "Guns?"

"We're mistaking the target, Admiral. We're hitting the weaker vessel."

"What do you mean, Guns?" Holland demanded.

"I think we're concentrating on the *Prinz Eugen* instead—" His urgent cry was drowned by the thunder of a great salvo striking the *Prince of Wales* half a mile away. The navy's newest battleship reeled and Vice-Admiral Holland knew she must have suffered serious damage. He flashed up his glasses, ignoring

Guns for a moment. Around him his staff officers tensed as signals started to fly back and forth between the two great ships.

"Bridge hit," someone read off the aldis lamp signal, as a yeoman on the *Prince of Wales* clicked his machine on and off. "Shambles . . . severe casualties . . . Captain Leach and . . . Chief Yeoman of Signals . . . only survivors . . . Turrets still operational . . ." As if to confirm the signal, cherry-red flame speckled the thick smoke rising from the bent, twisted, wrecked bridge. A turret had crackled into action once more.

The sight galvanised Holland into renewed action. "What did you say, Guns?"

"Wrong target, sir. We're going for the *Prinz Eugen*."

"Switch targets to the *Bismarck*," Holland rasped urgently. "Now!" They should not have continued to attack the *Prinz Eugen* for so long.

"But sir, we're having trouble – technical trouble."

Holland could have groaned out loud, but he knew a successful commander never reveals his feelings to his subordinates. Instead he barked, "What? Quick!"

"Breakdowns, sir. We didn't have time enough to work them up after the last refit."

Refit! The word stabbed Holland in the heart. It was the same old thing. It was the failing that successive captains of the *Hood* must have heard time and time again over the last quarter of a century of the ship's life.

"Don't worry, sir," Guns reassured him urgently. "We've still got the workmen on board. I'm getting them cracking on the problem tootsweet. For dockies they're good lads. They're going all out. But they are civvies." He raised his voice and tried to cheer the Admiral up. "God knows, sir, what the unions'll say about all this. You know how bolshy they are at the—"

"Get to it. Fire with what you've got, Guns."

"Yessir." The tube went dead.

Time was running out fast. The *Hood* had eight more minutes to live . . .

The *Prinz Eugen*'s guns roared. The grey sky was ripped apart by their elemental fury. One . . . two . . . three huge spouts of whirling water flailed upwards. The men on the *Eugen*'s bridge caught their breath. None of the Tommies could survive that elemental fury, that lethal maelstrom of deadly steel and fire.

Collectively they gasped. A lone destroyer, rocked by the shells from side to side, was coming straight at the 19,000-ton battleship. Time and time again, her ragged, shrapnel-torn masts seemed to touch the very water. But she remained stubbornly afloat, intent on her mission of death.

The side machine guns and light 20mm quick-firers took up the new challenge. A solid wall of white fire erupted on the *Prinz Eugen*'s starboard side. No one, it seemed, could live through that murderous fire. The lone destroyer disappeared into the smoke of battle. But no! There she was again, smoke pouring furiously from her twin funnels, reeling drunkenly from side to side as she was buffeted relentlessly by that terrific rate of fire. It lashed her as if to her doom, time and time again. But still she survived, as if by magic, though she sank visibly as she did so.

Sink the Hood

Clasped together like orphans in the storm, soaked with the foam and the great splashes of sea water that were thrown over the side of the *Prinz Eugen*, Hansen and Klaus stared in disbelief at their puny attackers. "Only madmen can do anything like that," Klaus roared, eyes full of the tragedy in the making, the sea water streaming down his face like bitter salt tears.

"They're half dead already," Hansen roared back in a voice that Klaus could hardly recognise. "It ain't human . . . *Himmelherrje*, how in God's name do they survive?"

But perhaps even God was no longer capable of logical thought that terrible May. Perhaps He wasn't even thinking; had given up on these mad creatures below who knew no sense, no reason, carried away as they were by that crazy unreasoning anti-logic of total war.

Now the destroyer, smoke pouring from her wrecked aft bow, losing speed visibly, was only a matter of a couple of hundred metres away. Even without realising it logically, Klaus von Kadowitz knew the Tommy was going to ram the mighty battleship. It would achieve nothing, save perhaps to slow the *Prinz Eugen* down a few knots. But it would be a last symbol of defiance. The Tommies, under that polite, calm exterior of theirs, were tough, obstinate bastards. They didn't give up.

So he let what had to happen happen. What could he do about it anyway? All around, all those except for the gunners, who continued to blast away in elemental fury, ripping great chunks of metal from the doomed craft, tearing her apart visibly, did the same. They watched with hypnotised fascination.

197

Now Klaus could see everything about her with utter clarity: the fallen masts, the shattered bridge, the shrapnel-torn funnels, the dead lying everywhere like bundles of abandoned soaked rags. It was as if a ghost ship from one of the ancient Nordic sagas was advancing on the *Prinz Eugen* out of exact revenge for some unknown age-old slight.

Then it happened.

Frustrated beyond all measure, the gunnery officer in charge of the deck bellowed through his phone to the score of gun-layers crouched the length of the *Prinz Eugen* and sweating, despite the icy cold, "Full salvo . . . FIRE AT WILL!"

The gunners, up to their ankles in empty shell cases, cartridge cases piled up to left and right, abandoned machine gun belts thrown in heaps like nests of curled snakes, needed no urging. They were afraid and exhausted. If they were going to die, then let it happen. If they weren't, then they wanted to destroy the bastard stubborn Tommy *now* – get the ordeal over with at last.

They took final aim. All rules learned on the musketry ranges so long before were thrown to the winds. They were out to kill – destroy – tear apart – completely destruct. Make this dying nemesis disappear at last. The whole side of the *Prinz Eugen* facing the Tommy destroyer, towering up above the dying craft like a mighty steel cliff, erupted. In an instant all was a mass of brilliant white and fiery red. Nothing could survive such an inhumane hail of fire.

But the Tommy ship, stopped in its tracks by that tremendous barrage, sinking rapidly, but without a single soul attempting to save himself, had one last trick to pull. She would be unable to ram the *Prinz Eugen* now, but there remained to her one final card. Her torpedoes!

Klaus saw it first. The flurry of bubbles. It was followed by the momentary silver gleam of the first torpedo speeding away from the dying craft.

"Enemy torpedo . . . starboard . . . bearing . . ." His voice trailed away to nothing. He couldn't be heard over that tremendous ear-splitting volume of fire.

Hansen heard, however. He grabbed Klaus even tighter. His fingers dug into the younger man's arm cruelly as the sweat, mixed with spray, streamed down his desperate scarlet face. It was the moment before Obermaat Hansen died. It was a moment that Klaus would remember for the rest of his life. Hansen's lips were moving. Was he saying a prayer? Or, more probably, was he cursing his fate? Klaus von Kadowitz never found out . . .

The torpedo slammed into the side of the *Prinz Eugen* the very next instant. The world exploded. Klaus felt Hansen wrenched from his arms and whirled into outer space by that great howling wind. Then he was gone – they all were. He was alone in a great howling red world, with the light vanishing rapidly and the enormous echoing roar that seemed to go on for ever and ever . . .

Nineteen

The *Prinz Eugen*'s second salvo came falling out of the flaming, smoke-filled sky. This time the shells didn't miss. The *Hood*'s main mast was hit. It came tumbling down in a mess of sparking wires and crumbling metal. Shrapnel hissed across the deck. Men were scythed down everywhere. Still the great battle-cruiser plunged on at top speed, apparently unaffected.

The second shell from the *Eugen* did it, however. On the deck, piled high because they had arrived too late and there was no immediate stowage available, the new, secret anti-aircraft shells exploded with a roar. Almost immediately a furious blaze broke out. The wind had sent a great blowtorch of all-consuming flame the whole length of that tremendous deck.

It was the target the *Bismarck* needed. Against that flame her major target, the *Hood*, was clearly outlined in stark detail. Lutjens didn't hesitate. He knew where to strike and there could be no excuse for the gunners: they simply couldn't miss, could they?

Swiftly Fire Control made their calculations. They relayed them to an impatient Lutjens, who was going to have the honour of issuing the decisive fire order himself. He'd go down in history after all. He looked at his reflection in the glass of the bridge proudly. Yes, he would be remembered as the officer who sank the *Hood*, the Pride of the English Navy.

Next moment he reeled, and just prevented himself from falling by grabbing a stanchion at the very last second. The *Bismarck* had been hit. Next to him a thick steaming stream of crimson blood was pouring on to the chart table from the tube. Around the chart table, the officers slumped back in their little chairs, unconscious or dead. The Tommies were fighting back. Now it was going to be a duel to the death.

Shaking his head, Lutjens, not realising that his white cap had gone and there was a thin stream of blood edging its way down the left side of his hard face, started to call out the fire order the best he could. The crew of the *Hood* had less than five minutes to live . . .

Through his glasses Lutjens surveyed the ship. Her captain was reacting. So far she had been able to use only half her firing power; her aft turrets were unable to fire. Now her skipper had brought her round and was beginning to fire on Lutjens' own flagship. He narrowed his gaze against the hell of flying steel and smoke to his front.

Every minute was now vital, the German commander told himself. The longer he was engaged in this battle, the more time the Tommies had to bring up the rest of their superior numbers. Once he had dealt with the *Hood*, he'd make a run for it. No one would question his decision after that particular triumph. For seconds he considered how to deal the *Hood* her death blow. Then he had it.

He knew now the state of the *Hood*'s armour in general and the fatal weakness of her steel deck. All that was needed was a single shell to penetrate that deck as far as the main magazine below. "In that moment," he said half aloud, while his officers stared at the trickle of blood as if mesmerised and waited for the admiral to make his final decision, "she'll be finished." The exploding magazine would blow her apart.

He made his decision. "Elevate A and B," he commanded. "Maximum height . . . plunging fire . . . two salvoes." He relaxed, the spirit seeming to flow from his lean hard body as if someone had opened an unseen tap. He had done all he could. Now everything depended upon the *Bismarck*'s gunners – and the rapacity and sloppiness of those English shipyard owners and their trade union officials of so long ago. "Carry on," he said – and that was that. He had made his last decision.

The great shells – one, two, three – plunged with devastating impact through the deck, igniting the anti-aircraft shells. The *Hood* commenced trembling – violently, frighteningly. The men caught by this strange movement trembled too. They looked as if they had been caught by some strange medieval plague, one of those which made men and women twitch, cry, engage in a parody of a leaping dance in the streets for no apparent reason. What was it?

On the cruiser *Norfolk* they viewed the sudden transformation of the sky – grey to violet, and then to grey once more – with bewilderment, too. What was going on? What was happening to the *Hood*?

Sink the Hood

The next instant they started to find out. Suddenly, startlingly, the grey sky turned to flame. The *Hood* gave a violent shudder. It was like that of some wild animal of the forest, caught by the hunter's bullet and taken by surprise as its hindlegs began to weaken and it started to fall for no apparent reason.

There was a hellish boom. Abruptly the *Hood* was shrouded by thick billowing smoke which reached higher and higher into the grey sky. Behind, there were gouts of vivid flame and a frightening trembling once more. The *Hood* began to come apart. The watchers gaped, open-mouthed and stupid in disbelief. Surely . . . not the *Hood*? their contorted faces seemed to say.

She was racked by yet another explosion. There was the ear-splitting grinding of metal being torn apart by force. Like some great whale surfacing for air, the whole of her bow rose higher and higher. Tiny figures slid from it. A man dived from a shattered derrick. He missed his aim, hit the deck like a sack of wet cement and burst open. Very faintly the watchers could, by straining their ears, hear the faint cries for *help, mercy, mother*!

Abruptly the bow plunged down again. A spout of whirling white water appeared as the bow started to sink. More and more panic-stricken ratings flung themselves into the freezing, killing water. They wouldn't last more than a couple of minutes. Now the men of the *Hood* were beginning to die by the score, the hundred, the thousand. All hope had vanished.

On the *Norfolk* the watchers turned their heads, eyes filled with tears. They could bear to observe the tragedy no longer. Their shipmates, men they had trained with,

203

drunk with, visited brothels with in the Middle East and the China Seas, were dying only a mile or two away – and there was absolutely nothing they could do about it.

Another German salvo thundered. Again the *Norfolk*'s officers forced themselves to raise their binoculars to view the tragedy taking place before them. But there was no explosion. What had gone wrong? Were the Hun shells dud? Was the *Hood* going to be allowed to go to her watery grave in a final peace?

It was not to be. Admiral Lutjens had ensured his final order had been carried out to the letter. This time the *Hood* must go – and go for good. Then, not to put too fine a point on it, the *Bismarck* would flee for her very life.

"*Look!*" a young officer on the bridge of the *Norfolk* howled – a cry like the elemental one of some wild animal caught in a trap and in extremis. "For God's sake – LOOK!"

A violent sheet of purple flame shot hundreds of feet high. There was a tremendous crash which sent great combers heading towards the watching cruiser. Over forty-two thousand tons of defective steel, which had been the Pride of the British Navy's greatest secret – and her undoing – flew through the air. It all happened so fast that the men on the bridge of the *Norfolk* could hardly follow it.

Molten, red-hot metal started to shower the sea. It boiled in crazy fury. It set the oil leaking from the shattered tanks afire. Swiftly the tide of burning, flaming oil swept forward, engulfing the men attempting to brave the freezing water, catching up with the best swimmers and those on Carley floats in an instant. They screamed, as they too were turned into flaming torches: poor pathetic creatures, who screamed and pleaded with God for mercy in their last few seconds alive. But there was no mercy from the grey unfeeling heavens. God was – on this day – looking the other way.

A vast cloud of thick black smoke now arose.

It gave those silent men on the bridge of the *Norfolk* a moment's respite from the horror. But they appeared mesmerised. They didn't move. They didn't speak. They were like cheap actors frozen into position at the close of a final act in some third-rate melodrama . . .

On the *Bismarck*, the victor, the crew went wild with joy. A wave of overwhelming ecstatic joy swept through the great battleship as deck after deck, right down to the engine room, learned of their triumph. Men embraced. Officers shook hands and fell on each other's shoulders like men who had not seen each other for years.

Momentarily the iron discipline of the Kriegsmarine broke down. Those who possessed illegal flatmen on duty broke them out and started toasting the victory. Others ran wildly, aimlessly, up and down the steel passages, shouting, yelling, punching shipmates heartily in the ribs. "Good old *Bismarck*!" they yelled, beside themselves with joy. "I knew she'd do it. That'll learn that drunken sot Churchill. Now he can go and stick his cigar up his own fat arse . . ."

Men started to sing. Others, already drunk on illegal schnapps and crazed exuberance, danced clumsily together while their comrades cheered, made obscene gestures, blew them wet kisses and maintained they were going to their bunks to "fetch up the vaseline, dreamboat!"

Up on the deck where they had watched the end of the *Hood* – for that pillar of smoke had now vanished to reveal an empty sea where the English ship had been – they cheered and cried, *"Heim zur Mutter, Jungs . . .* Parades and as much tin as you can carry on yer frigging heroic chest, mate. Flowers; girls; yes, girls being thrown at yer as if it's Christmas every frigging day . . . Oh, you frigging heroes, what a homecoming it's gonna be. *Heim zur Mutter, Jungs!*"

For his part, Admiral Lutjens no longer shared the joy of his crew. The triumph was over almost as soon as he had felt it at the disappearance of the *Hood*. The fate of the great enemy ship had made him realise that the same one could overtake the *Bismarck*, too.

At six thirty-two a.m., at the moment of his victory, he had signalled Raeder in Berlin: 'Have sunk battle-cruiser, probably *Hood*. Another battleship damaged and in retreat. Two heavy cruisers are shadowing us. Fleet Commander.'

Half an hour later, at five past seven, his moment of exhilaration vanished to be replaced by one of despondency and foreboding. He signalled his chief once more. By this time his sense of triumph at his great victory over the English had vanished totally. The message was sombre. It read:

1. Engine Room Four out of action.
2. Port stoke-hold leaking, but can be held. Bows leaking severely.

3. Cannot make more than eighteen knots.
4. Two enemy radio scanners observed.
5. Intend to run to St Nazaire. No loss of men.
Fleet Commander.

The crazy intoxication of victory was over. Cold reality took over as the admiral realised what was now to come. The English wouldn't give up; they never did. The Tommies had long memories. They had been temporarily defeated – but now their admirals, their governors and, above all, their people would demand revenge at all costs. He had to escape while there was still time – or else . . . But the doomed Admiral Lutjens dare not think that tremendous, overwhelming thought to its logical conclusion.

Majestically the *Bismarck* sailed on to her own fate. Behind her she left the sea empty, tossing back and forth in that green, cold immensity, save for the mass of floating debris – and the lone man from the *Hood* on the Carley rubber float, sobbing as if his very heart was broken.

Envoi

The mood in the Gay Hussar was sombre that lunchtime. Outside the sky over London was leaden and threatening. There was a hint of snow in the air. People walked by hunched against the cold. Newspaper sellers huddled in front of braziers next to the meths drinkers. Their posters read 'Euro Crashes . . . EC Panic Measures!'

Just inside the door, Lord Longford was talking earnestly at the small 'single' table to some unfortunate. Closer to the centre of the inner room, a well-known ex-Labour cabinet minister, huddled in a camel-hair coat for some reason, was complaining bitterly to a publishing gent that the tenth volume of his memoirs of a working-class boyhood in Yorkshire wasn't selling well. It was the same as usual except that the plaque commemorating the old Seventy-Eight Division belonging to the 'Hungarian' from Dewsbury who had founded the Gay Hussar was missing. It had been the last link with the place's past save for the *gulyas*, hot, steaming and full of chunks of pork and beef, that my publisher was tucking into heartily.

He was making one of his fleeting visits to the UK –

he followed the MCC cricket around the world for most of the season – and he enjoyed what he called 'typical English grub'. Obviously he'd never been into a typical English McDonald's.

"So you solved the mystery in the end, Duncan," he said, reaching for the red wine – Tokay, naturally. "The mystery of what really happened to HMS *Hood*."

"I suppose so," I answered hesitantly. I wasn't quite sure I had. But it didn't really matter now, did it? All that mattered was to build a small and transitory memorial in words to these dead men of so long ago.

The publisher took my answer for agreement. "Splendid," he said, spearing another big chunk of soft pork, the thick gravy dripping from it – rather nauseatingly, in my opinion. "Our readers do like their 'faction' to be accurate, you know, Duncan. They're an eagle-eyed lot. They know their Mark Ones from their Mark Twos. You can't fool our chaps." He swallowed the pork chunk and beamed at me, as if he were exceedingly proud of 'our' readers. "It's like at cricket, you know. These modern umpires would get away with murder if it weren't for the old hands who watch them like hawks. Naturally they know their rule books – and *Wisden* – back to front. So—"

"Surprisingly enough," I cut in rudely – I am not one bit interested in cricket; the only thing I have noticed about it, since the day I gratefully turned in my pads when I left school, is that the players seem to wear a lot of make-up now, which certainly wasn't in when I was habitually bowled out for a duck – "I found what I suppose you'd call the last piece of the jigsaw here in London. It was when I was here to see Horace the Obit—"

"Who?" my publisher asked, removing some tough meat fragments from his excellent capped teeth – after all, *he* can afford good teeth, can't he? "Who did you say?"

"Please forget it. It doesn't matter. But I chanced upon him—"

"This Horace chap?"

"*No*, the last piece of the jigsaw – at King's Cross just before setting off for the North."

"Oh, the North," he echoed dully, as if I'd mentioned I'd been setting off for an expedition to the Arctic Circle. "Headingly's in the North, isn't it?"

I ignored the reference to the well-known Leeds cricket ground and said, "I could see he was blind even before he spoke. It was the patch he was wearing on his right sleeve together with the white cane."

My publisher had already lost interest, and was searching for another piece of pork to spear with his fork. Obviously it was a task that took a great deal of care and concentration, even for a publisher whose readers were skilled enough to know all about Mark Ones and Mark Twos.

The foreigner was tall, handsome in an old-fashioned way, wearing his hair sleeked back rather like Prince Philip and those other survivors of the old German aristocracy. His guide was much younger and looking worried, as if he were concerned that the old man wearing the yellow patch of the war-blinded on his sleeve might not make it on his own in a very crowded King's Cross.

The foreigner didn't seem one bit concerned, on the other hand. He kept patting his guide's hand reassuringly and whispering, "*Schon gut, schon gut. Ich schaff' das schon, altes Haus. Schon gut . . .*"

I didn't discover his profession – *vocation* might be a better word – until he had entered the carriage, said, "*Guten Abend*," to everyone in an old-fashioned German manner and sat down opposite me, asking in English, "I can smoke?"

"*Ja, Sie können rauchen, Herr Pfaffer,*" I answered, showing off as usual and addressing him as 'pastor', for that seemed to be what he was. At least, he was wearing the German Lutheran equivalent of the dog-collar black sweater with a tieless white shirt, its long lapels hanging over the edge of the pullover.

His face lit up – it made him look at least ten years younger – and he bowed stiffly, again in that old-fashioned German style, saying, "Klaus von Kadowitz. *Ich fahre nach Hull . . . Seemanns Mission, verstehen Sie?*"

"The ice had been broken," I told my publisher, "and by an amazing coincidence I'd met an eyewitness, dressed as a German clergyman, nearly sixty years after the event."

My publisher wasn't particularly impressed. Like all Londoners and ex-public schoolboys, he had spent long years being trained not to show surprise – just, as you might phrase it, qualified and somewhat reserved interest.

211

"I say," he commented, savouring his latest piece of pork, "that was quite a turn up for the books, eh. Jolly interesting." He got down to what he called his 'vittles' once more. "What happened then, Duncan?"

I hesitated. What was the use?

But just then Leo came through the door, leaning on an elegant silver-topped cane and looking more like the Squire of Stroud than ever. He gave me an encouraging smile and shrugged. It meant 'Soldier on, old chap. It might never happen' or something of that sort. He sat down and I turned back to my publisher and my account of this strange, totally unexpected meeting at King's Cross and what followed after that.

"You see, he was some kind of travelling pastor, whose job it was to visit German seaman's missions abroad. He was on his way to the one at Hull, just outside King George's Dock, where the ferries to Holland and Belgium go from." I knew the detail didn't interest my publisher one bit – nothing north of the Wash ever did – but I felt constrained to put him in the picture. Authors are expected to put in the details; it's part of their job. "He'd hold a service there, distribute a few Bibles, have a beer to be matey and one of the chaps, console some poor miserable sod whose wife had left him—"

My publisher pushed away his plate and started eyeing the dessert trolley, hoping, presumably, there'd be some of those overly rich and creamy Austro-Hungarian *torten*, which old-fashioned Continentals – and English people – still eat in this weight-conscious age.

I repressed a sigh, waved to Leo, who was saying goodbye to Lord Longford, and added, "Just outside

Peterborough, when we'd broken the ice and he knew what I was writing, he told me about the *Prinz Eugen* and the metal. It was the secret revealed at last . . ."

By now Klaus von Kadowitz knew he was blind. One Ball, his fellow patient in the surgical ward, had tried hard to get him to see more than a shadowy outline. He'd crept back and forth from his bed, tenderly holding the wad of bandages which protected his remaining testicle – he'd lost the other, and nearly his life, in the freezing sea after the *Bismarck* had been sent to the bottom by the Tommies – urging Klaus to shout when he could see his outline. But in the end, when Oberschwester Klara had severely ordered One Ball back to the bed with the blood-filled chamberpot beneath it, they had conceded that the explosion which had killed Obermaat Hansen had virtually blinded him.

"Don't worry, Klaus," One Ball had repeatedly tried to console him during those first bitter days after that overwhelming realisation. Plenty of girls ready to oblige wounded war heroes like us."

In later years when he was studying theology at Kiel University, Klaus had often thought of One Ball, who had been killed two years later during the great week-long raids on Hamburg in 1943. One Ball had seen him through the worst time. He had made Klaus come to terms with his horrific injury and made him realise that he still had a life in front of him. Indeed, it had turned out to be a long, happy one with a loving wife – that same Oberschwester Klara, who had seemed to be so strict – and a supportive ministry out in the Frisian Islands, where they understood the ways of men who had once gone out to sea.

Some time that summer, One Ball proclaimed quite happily, "Listen, Klaus, the big shots are coming to hang medals on our manly breasts." He had lowered his voice as if he were imparting a state secret to Klaus, sitting on the white chair near the open window of the ward, enjoying the summer sun's rays on his face. "The buzz among the nurses is that the Führer *himself* is coming – and the ceremony is going to be filmed for posterity by the Deutsche Wochenschau! *Now* what do you say to that, Old House? Klaus, old friend, we've hit the jackpot!"

They hadn't. All the same, the Führer did appear, as the rumour had said he would. He didn't stay long. He had never liked the northern ports. But Admiral Raeder had convinced him that he had to travel from the new Russian front, which was now his primary interest, to boost the morale of the navy after the sinking of the *Bismarck*. So he went through his usual act for the cameras of the Deutsche Wochenschau: a smile, a serious look, the production of the Iron Cross, a close-up of him bending down over the wounded hero in his blue-and-white striped hospital pyjamas, the medal pinned on, the hand clasped, a pat on the cheek and on to the next hero who had spent his blood for 'Folk, Fatherland and Führer'.

"I received the same treatment," the pastor confided to me as we sped through Peterborough heading north. "Iron Cross, First Class – lost it years ago. Nazi medals are not much prized in post-war Germany," Pastor von Kadowitz added with a wry grin on his old face. "Plus I got one

214

of his three standard phrases for the wounded. In my case it was, 'Keep your ears stiff, Ensign,' and then he was gone with his entourage stamping after him, all heavy boots and clanking swords and medals and poor old One Ball moaning, 'For God's sake, *doucement, doucement* . . . all that shitting stamping makes my shitting afflicted appendage ache!' He smiled softly at me. "Poor chap, he never did learn to moderate his language once he was a civvie again."

I reflected a moment or two. How strange. Here was a man who had received a medal for bravery from the arch-tyrant himself, sitting among unsuspecting Standard Class passengers, snoring, reading the latest Jilly Cooper – God bless her – or eating Great Northern Railways' excellent – if expensive – tuna-and-cress sandwiches. Funny old world, there was no denying it.

"Afterwards, when the Führer had gone," he had continued, "Grand Admiral Raeder, no less, had made an appearance to see me *personally.*"

"The head of the German Navy?"

"The same."

Suddenly I realised that I was on the verge of an explanation for the great mystery of the *Hood*. I don't know how or why. I just knew it . . . like a vision. I tensed and waited.

"He exchanged the usual civilities for a political sailor – which he was – but," Klaus von Kadowitz explained, "I felt he was visiting me because he really felt something for me and – I hope – all the rest of us who had suffered in the *Bismarck* fiasco. You know he was a stiff, unbending sort of person with that old-fashioned

215

manner and uniform of his. But I sensed he wanted to
explain why I'd lost—" He didn't finish the sentence,
but I knew what he meant.

"Go on," I urged.

"Well, to cut a long story short, Mr Harding, he
produced a lump of metal. It was from the *Hood*, he
explained. Naturally I couldn't see it. So he handed it
to me and said, 'Feel it, Oberfahnrich.'"

"And?"

"I did so . . . quite puzzled, wondering why he had
broken away from the Führer's party to see me and
give me a piece of metal from the *Hood*. It meant
nothing to me until he commanded, 'Feel it again
and tell me what the surface of the rough edge feels
like.'"

"And what had it felt like?" I interjected, leaning
forward urgently, realising that I was now almost at
the end of the trail.

Even in the eminently level-headed environment of the
Gay Hussar I wasn't altogether able to contain the note
of excitement in my voice and my publisher exclaimed
with the fake enthusiasm of a boy from a good school
who had been trained always to repress his feelings, "I
say, how jolly exciting!" He dipped his cake fork into
the Sachertorte almost as if with regret that he was
destroying that beautiful balance of cream and cake.
"Go on, Duncan."

"Well, according to the German pastor, it was not only
rough but porous and pitted." I groped hurriedly for a
simile to make my meaning quite clear. "You know, a

bit like those Aero chocolate bars made by Rowntrees in the old days."

"They still make them, Duncan. Now and again I indulge. Memories of school and all that." He slid his cake fork once more into the crumbling edifice of that Austrian concoction before it tumbled down in complete ruin.

"So the *Hood*'s armour had been virtually worthless. The Pride of the British Navy – even the British Empire – had been based on a ship which successive governments in the twenties and thirties – naturally with the connivance of the factory owners and labour union bosses; they didn't want to blow the whistle and lose jobs for their members during the Depression – had shored up with cheap, inferior steel – no match for that being turned out by Germany's Ruhr Barons." I took a hasty sip of my wine, feeling myself flush even more.

Across the way, Leo waved his fork at me. Was it a warning?

With a flourish, my publisher finished the last of his torte and gave a contented sigh. "Makes a good punchline," he commented, as if he were suddenly very tired. "Mind you, this is not fact but fiction you're writing, Duncan. But it's a nice symbol. A crumbling Empire protects itself with a great ship that is crumbling as well. Not bad." He cocked his head to one side in that chirpy manner of his which he uses to make clear to his authors that he is assessing them. "What of the Jerry?"

"You mean the pastor . . . Klaus von Kadowitz?"

"Yes." He had dropped his gaze and was staring at the satellite TV cricket schedules which he carried around with him all the time. His interest had vanished already.

I shrugged. "He changed at Doncaster," I answered baldly. After all, what did it matter? Nothing much does.

Five minutes later we'd shaken hands, he'd muttered something about looking forward to the 'latest opus' and that a cheque was 'in the post' – they always are, aren't they – and hurried off, presumably to watch cricket from Brisbane or somewhere or other.

Leo saw me rise to follow. He signalled, 'A snifter for the Road to the Isles?' He meant Yorkshire. He was a Yorkshireman himself, but he always made out that Yorkshire was some remote province that could only be reached by dog sledge and huskies.

I nodded.

Leo's 'snifters' usually come in triple glasses. But it didn't matter much. They could pour me into the three o'clock for Aberdeen at King's Cross. It's usually full of drunken Scots anyway. One more lush wouldn't be noticed.

We toasted. Leo signalled discreetly for another. He was the most generous of publishers I've ever known, and I've known the breed now ever since I wrote my first book as an undergraduate. "Why do you do it, Duncan?"

"You mean novels?"

"Yes; they're not of importance. It's not like your non-fiction."

I shrugged. "Search me, Leo." I used the phrase of my youth. "Perhaps you can say things in novels that you can't in non-fiction."

The second snifter arrived. It looked even bigger. Leo raised his glass in toast.

I swallowed it in a gulp. "Let me say this, Leo," I said, swaying slightly as I rose.

"Say on, old friend Duncan."

"Someone's got to write books for women in pinnies, who lost sons in wars long forgotten."

"Here's to women in pinnies – whatever they are." Leo drained the rest of his snifter.

I ignored my old friend. "Women who wear men's boots cut at the side on account of their corns."

"Very obscure, Duncan. But I'm sure you know what you're talking about."

I wasn't offended. No one ever can be with Leo. Besides, I must have sounded an awful 'arse with ears', as the unlamented late Obermaat Hansen might have said.

"Bye," I said and staggered outside, leaving my old friend mystified. I started waving frantically for a taxi – I usually do after a 'publisher's lunch', which ends by being very liquid. I prayed I'd find one which would deliver me to King's Cross and the 'Road to the Isles'. On the morrow I'd begin another epic . . .